Blackmail

Hilda Stahl

Cover Illustration by Ed French

DEDICATED WITH LOVE
to the Gerbers
Dan, Becki, Aaron, Brandy
Joe & Scott

Chapter 1

Amber Ainslie gripped the steering wheel as she turned off the expressway on the Chambers exit. Music from a Phil Driscoll tape filled the car. Wind blew and the gray overcast sky once again threatened rain. She thought about the terrible case she was working on and her stomach knotted painfully.

"Heavenly Father, help me track down the lead on this kiddy porn outfit," she prayed as she picked up speed. "Thank you for special discernment and wisdom in dealing with these people so I can recognize the truth no matter what they say. And protect those three little kids they're using. Help me find them quickly."

Tears burned Amber's eyes as she slowed for a traffic signal. Her red mass of curls tumbled over her shoulders and down her back. Of all the cases she had experienced, this had to be the worst emotionally. How could anyone subject children to the things her client had told her? Was it possible that the head guy did, indeed, live in Chambers? After telling her friend, Sheriff Fritz Javor, what she knew, he gave her more details learned from a photographer, Jaz Knobb, who had been arrested yesterday. The man had willingly told who hired him—Perkins Weese, a sleeze who would take a porn picture or a video of anyone for a price. When he needed an extra photographer he hired Jaz Knobb.

"Amber, I shouldn't be telling you confidential information. But I don't have jurisdiction in Chambers," Fritz had said.

"Since I'm a private investigator I can go anywhere," said Amber with a nod.

"You got it, Red."

"I want to get these people bad, Fritz."

"You be careful. You'll be out there playing with some mighty big boys in this one."

"People are sick," she said. "Sick!"

"That they are," he agreed.

The light changed and she drove to Crest Street and turned right. This was one case she wanted to blow wide open. The police were working on it too, but they didn't have the freedom that she had. They couldn't arrest anyone until they had proof. She intended to find that proof, put a stop to the kiddy porn ring and send the top guys to prison to rot.

Could she find the three kids her client had told her about before they were subjected to more abuse?

She drove past Palma Christian Center and wished she could stop in for church, but knew she couldn't today. She had an appointment with a couple of men who insisted this was the only time they could talk to her.

What if they knew where the three kids were hidden? Maybe they would give her the lead she needed to find the top guy.

"Heavenly Father, thank you for your help. You're always with me and I thank you for that too."

* * *

Several miles away ten-year-old Carlie peeked around the door. A man was talking to the woman Carlie called Ma. Ma and the man were sitting at the kitchen table with cups of coffee. Ma had sent Carlie out for a walk but she sneaked back in to listen. She knew they were going to talk about her. But what would they say? Maybe the man knew her real family. For all the years she lived with Ma, Carlie knew the woman wasn't really any relation to her.

Many times Carlie had asked, "Why can't I live with my own mom and dad?"

Ma had said, "It don't pay to ask dumb questions. You're here with me and that's where you'll stay until something better comes along."

Carlie frowned and tugged her snagged sweater down over her faded jeans. Was this 'the better' that Ma was always talking about?

"I say she's worth more than that, Perkins," Ma said gruffly. "You're trying to get her for nothing."

Perkins took a swig of coffee and plunked his cup down. "You think so, huh?"

"She's a pretty little thing and we both know it," said Ma. "You'll make a fortune off Carlie."

Carlie shivered. Ma intended to sell her to this man, Perkins! But why would he want to buy her?

Finally Perkins named a price Ma agreed on and he handed over the money. Ma chuckled and counted it again, then again.

Her heart hammering, Carlie eased away from the door and tip-toed to the window she'd climbed through. Where could she hide so they wouldn't find her?

***

Sara Noreen Palmer sat in her usual spot in Palma Christian Center, five rows from the platform and on the left side of the wide building. Soft piano and organ music covered the whispers of the congregation. The perfume of the woman in front of her was pleasant and she considered asking her what it was. The woman was a stranger, so she didn't ask. Sara crossed her long legs and smoothed her soft wool skirt over her knees. She laid her Bible and her black leather purse beside her where Roger usually sat. She flipped her long chestnut-brown hair over the shoulder of her blue wool jacket. It felt strange without Roger beside her. She had been on a two-week business trip with Rita Hardy and he was away with his parents today. Their agreement was to finally talk seriously about getting married after her return.

The organ and piano music swelled, then quieted as three men walked from a side door to the spacious platform. Bright spring flowers and green ferns decorated the area near the choir loft. Lazily Sara watched the men, then her eyes riveted on the tall man in the middle as he sat on the velvet padded guest speaker's chair, his Bible in his large, sun-browned hands. A shock passed through her and her mouth turned bone dry. Her ears buzzed and the room spun as she locked her icy hands together in her lap.

After eight years could he really just pop up in her life?

Was it Boyd Collier sitting on the platform or someone who looked like him?

During the opening prayer she stared at him, her stomach a hard, cold knot. His sable brown hair was combed back off his wide forehead instead of flopping across it as it had in the past. Sooty lashes brushed his cheeks and his mouth moved in silent prayer. His jaw was strong and she remembered its stubborn set. His nose was too long to be called classic. She recalled teasing him about it just to make him angry.

Sara caught her trembling red lip between her teeth. She was twenty-five and he was six years older, so that made him thirty-one. Was he married? Did he have children? She couldn't see if he wore a wedding band.

Anger, embarrassment, curiosity, attraction, and then consuming rage washed over her in waves. How dare Boyd Collier suddenly appear in her well-ordered life?

She had to walk out before Boyd saw her, but she couldn't force enough strength in her legs.

What if Roger had been home this weekend to sit beside her? He'd guess that something was wrong and would probe until he learned the terrible truth about her past.

Pastor Ted Sawyer lifted his head and smiled at the congregation. "I want to introduce a new member of our church and our community. Boyd Collier. Many of us have read his wonderful, inspirational books."

Sara bit back a groan. It was Boyd Collier! New church member? New in the community? And he wrote! Why hadn't she known that since she was a writer too?

"Boyd has bought a home just outside of Chambers and is in the process of moving in." Pastor Sawyer smiled at Boyd and Sara's heart sank even lower. "He transferred his membership from the church in Green Lake to here. Please welcome Boyd Collier as part of our family."

Boyd stood beside Pastor Sawyer and smiled. "It's a pleasure to be here in Palma Christian Center and to be a part of this community."

His deep voice echoed inside Sara, stirring a response that startled her. How she wanted to run but, if she moved, he would see her and then she felt as if she might never move again.

Smiling, Pastor Sawyer clasped Boyd's hand as he turned to the congregation. "After the service, greet Boyd and make him feel welcome. If you've not had an opportunity to read his books, then stop at the back of the church where I've set up a table with several copies. He's agreed to autograph them if you'd like." Pastor turned back to Boyd. "We're proud to have you join us."

"Thank you. I'm glad to be here." Boyd smiled at

the pastor and then turned to flash another smile at the congregation. He glanced in Sara's direction and her heart almost stopped.

As he sat down again Sara sank low in her seat. How could she survive with Boyd Collier attending the same church, living in the same town, maybe even making the same friends?

The music of the song service rose around her, but she couldn't force words past the lump in her throat.

What could she do? She couldn't sell her precious house that she was buying with the income from her four juvenile fiction books. And she *wouldn't* give up her job as secretary to Rita Hardy—the income that kept her going between royalty checks.

She tried to listen as the pastor read the Scripture and started his sermon, but her thoughts shot back to when she was sixteen and first met Boyd and his family.

Sara had walked into the Collier living room between Mary and Jason Collier. The room was clean and pretty and not at all what she was used to. Mary had smiled and slipped her arm around Sara. "Boyd, I want you to meet our foster daughter, Sara Palmer. Sara, I told you about our son."

Sara knew Mary and Jason were happy to have her, but she could see by Boyd's face that he was upset.

"Hi, Sara," said Boyd with a smile that didn't reach his steel grey eyes. "I hope you like it here."

She flipped her tangled hair over her thin shoulder and looped her thumbs in her faded jeans pockets. She wore a dirty yellow tee shirt that she'd taken from her younger brother, Tim. She knew it was too tight but she didn't care. "I guess this is as good a place as any to live since I gotta live somewhere."

Boyd frowned. "You should be thankful that you're here."

She scowled.

"We're thankful that you're here, Sara," said Mary. "You'll keep Jason and me from being so lonely. Boyd's been away at college and this summer he's going to California to work."

Boyd shook his head. "Mother, Steve called just before you came in to tell me the job fell through. I'll have to stay right here to get a job. If you don't mind."

"Mind! Oh, Boyd, I'm so glad!" Mary hugged him tight and Sara clamped her lips together to hold back the angry remark.

"The job is still open at my place," said Jason smiling at Boyd.

"Thanks, Dad."

Sara watched them together with her eyes narrowed. They were nothing like her family. Her stepdad beat her, her mom drank and her brothers were always in trouble. Only Rosalee had it together, but then she was fourteen and not yet interested in boys. Sara inched behind a chair. Living with the Colliers would be better than at home, but it would take some adjustment.

"I'll show you your room, Sara," Mary said as

she caught Sara's hand and tugged her down a carpeted hallway to a small room with pink and white flowered wallpaper.

Sara looked around the room in awe, then turned suspiciously to Mary. "Who do I share it with?"

"No one."

"You got other foster kids?"

"Just you."

Sara looked around the clean room and suddenly felt dirty and out of place. "Boyd don't like me."

"Of course he does!"

"Well, I don't like him." She dropped to a chair near a small desk and looked out the window at the wide back yard where the summer sun shone on bright flowers. "I don't like him at all!"

"I'm sorry about that. I'm sure you'll learn to."

"I don't know about that. Does he know my ma kicked me out?"

"Yes."

Sara picked at the hole in the knee of her jeans. "Does he know about . . . about . . . you know."

"The baby?"

Sara nodded.

"No. I told you we wouldn't tell anyone unless you wanted it told."

"He'd probably hate me more if he knew I had a baby."

"Boyd is very kindhearted."

"Yah, sure." Sara jumped up and caught a glimpse of herself in the mirror. She looked ugly and dirty. "It was probably a good thing Ma took Carlie away. What would I do with a baby girl? Me! I sure wouldn't want no kid to grow up like me."

Mary slipped her arms aound Sara. Sara stiffened, but fought against sudden tears that pricked her eyes. She smelled Mary's special smell that was very different from Ma's.

"Sara, I want you to be happy. Jesus loves you and he wants you to be happy too. He sent you to us."

"Yah, sure."

Mary kissed Sara's cheek, then walked to the door. "The bathroom is right across the hall. And your closet has some clothes that I bought for you when I knew you'd be living here with us. And in the dresser too."

"I won't wear no dress!" Sara flung open the closet, but found only two dresses and a few blouses and tee shirts as well as a new pair of sneakers. In the dresser she found underwear and jeans and a thick red sweater. She wanted to hug all the new things to her, but she kept her back stiff and a scowl on her face as she turned back to Mary.

"Sara, I need you to be with me to pick out dress shoes."

"Why would I need more than sneakers?"

"For church."

Sara frowned.

"Remember, you agreed to go with us."

"Yah, sure."

The following Sunday she showered and, for the first time she could remember, dressed in a dress and shoes other than sneakers. It had been very strange going to church with the Colliers.

That first summer she saw Boyd often, but he ignored her most of the time. After he left for college, she'd relaxed and tried to fit into the Collier home. Mary had helped her with her manners, her speech and her physical appearance. Often she thought about her baby, Carlie, and wondered what she looked like and who was taking care of her. Several times she dreamed about Carlie. When she woke up she'd cry and long for her baby. She never told anyone about the dreams or the tears.

The summer she was seventeen Boyd had been home and he took her to church youth group parties and even the canoe trip. He had talked to her as if he cared about her and had even given her self-improvement books to study. That summer she accepted Jesus as her personal Savior and the whole family had rejoiced with her. Each time she thought of Carlie or dreamed about her, she'd pray for her. Knowing her prayers were helping her baby eased her pain a little. She never mentioned anything about Carlie. She hoped that Boyd would never learn about Carlie.

When Boyd left for his last year in college, she had cried herself to sleep for almost two months.

One Saturday in December she sat cross-legged on the living room floor watching TV alone when she heard a sound behind her. She turned to find Boyd home. She leaped up and flung herself against him. "Boyd!"

He hugged her close. "Hi, Sara."

She felt his heart thud against her and she pulled his face down and kissed him long and hard.

He pushed her away with a frown. "Don't do that, Sara!"

Tears flooded her eyes and she turned away.

"You can't kiss me like that and you know it."

A sob tore from her throat.

"Are you crying?" he asked gruffly.

She wanted to run from him, but her legs were too weak to support her.

"I didn't mean to hurt your feelings," he whispered.

She rubbed her eyes, but more tears fell.

"I am sorry, Sara." He gently turned her to him. "Please stop crying. I didn't mean to hurt you."

She crept into his arms and he held her. After a long time she lifted her face to him. "Boyd, I love you. I'll love you forever."

"Don't say that," he whispered hoarsely.

She touched his lips with the tip of her finger. "I want to marry you."

"You don't know what you want," he said hoarsely.

"I want you," she whispered.

He leaned down and kissed her, then with a strangled cry, jumped away from her. "Stop it, Sara!"

She held her hand out to him. "Please."

He groaned and slowly reached for her. Suddenly the phone rang and he jumped. He pushed her hand away. "Don't look at me like that! And don't you ever, ever talk to me about love!"

"I love you!"

"I don't love you!"

"Don't," she whispered.

"I would never love you or marry you! I know about you!"

Her heart froze in her breast. "What about me?"

"You had a baby!" He narrowed his eyes into steel slits. "I heard all about you, but I thought you'd changed. But you haven't! You'll never change! This proves it! I never want to see you again as long as I live. I will never return to this house while you live here!"

"You can't mean that!"

He savagely rubbed his mouth with the back of his hand. "I don't want to remember what happened here."

"I love you," she whimpered.

"When you graduate from high school, I want you out of here. Away from my home and my parents. And away from me! If you try to stay longer than that, I'll tell Mom what happened today."

"No, please."

"I will!"

Numbly she shook her head. He had gone on and on as she stood rooted to the carpet while his words struck blow after blow until love died and hatred for him filled and consumed her.

The hatred and anger burned stronger as she stared at the mature Boyd Collier who was listening to the sermon. She picked up her purse and gripped it until her fingers ached. She trembled, alarmed that her anger was still so strong. When she had left the Collier home at eighteen, she vowed silently never to contact them again even though she would miss

Mary and Jason and they'd miss her. When she decided on a career in writing she started to call Mary because Mary had first encouraged her interest in writing. But she backed out for fear Boyd might answer the phone and tell his mother the terrible story.

For the past four years she had lived in a small home she purchased in Chambers. She wrote Christian juvenile fiction under her first and middle names, Sara Noreen. When her first book was published, she picked up the phone to call Mary but couldn't find the courage.

Now she had her own friends and soon she would be engaged to Roger Cairns. She had four books on the market and they were doing exceptionally well. She was loved by many people. None of them knew about her past and she wanted it to stay that way.

She glanced at Boyd and pressed her lips tightly together. How long would it be before he told everyone all about her?

Chapter 2

A cold shiver ran down Sara's spine as Pastor Ted Sawyer closed in prayer. She had to get away fast before Boyd saw her. She turned to slip from the pew just as someone touched her arm. She jumped and bit back a scream. Slowly she turned to see her best friend, Neddie Jagger. "You scared me, girl," she said, forcing a laugh.

"Are you all right, Sara? You're as white as my blouse."

"I'm just tired, Neddie."

Neddie pushed her glasses up in place on her nose. Her blond hair was cut short and curled around her face. She was almost a head shorter than Sara, slender and attractive. "I've told you working even part-time for Mrs. Hardy and writing as much as you do will catch up with you. Rita Hardy can run ten people ragged."

Sara chuckled. "I know. But I'll be all right once I get home and rest. These two weeks with Rita were very tiring."

"Did you walk today?" Neddie knew how much Sara loved walking, especially during the brisk spring weather. Sara had an old car that ran quite well, but she walked as often as she could.

Sara nodded. She glanced quickly around but couldn't see Boyd. People milled around, visiting as they walked toward the door.

"Let me drive you home. I hear the wind blowing hard and it just might rain."

"Thanks, Neddie. I'd appreciate a ride." Sara managed a smile. "You're a good friend."

Neddie flushed and moved her purse from one hand to another. She hoped Sara never saw what was in her heart. "Someone has to take care of you with Roger out of town."

Sara pushed her hair back. "What would I do without you?"

"I want to speak to Boyd Collier first and then I'll be right with you. I'd really like to get to know that man. His books are remarkable."

Sara's stomach knotted painfully. "I'll wait in your car for you."

"I'd think you would want to meet Boyd Collier since you're both authors."

"Another time," Sara said stiffly. She pulled her jacket closed and moved restlessly from one high heel to another. "I really can walk if you want to stay to talk."

"Don't worry about it. I'll just introduce myself, welcome him and then we'll go. He is *so* handsome!"

Jealousy unexpectedly shot through Sara. "He's probably married," she snapped.

"No. I already asked," said Neddie with a mischievous grin.

Sara's pulse leaped and she abruptly turned away. "I'll wait in your car, Neddie."

"Be there soon."

Sara walked around two men, her ears ringing. She spotted Boyd near the door and quickly ducked around a crowd near his book table. Her legs trembled, but she forced herself to keep walking to the coat rack for her coat. She pulled it on and slipped out the wide front doors. Wind whipped her hair around her head and shoulders and blew her coattail around her legs. She found Neddie's car and gratefully slipped inside. It smelled of Neddie's perfume. Four blocks in this wind would have been too much.

Sara leaned back with a tired sigh. A little girl skipped past the car, laughing into the wind. Sara suddenly thought of Carlie. She'd be ten years old now. Was she happy? Was she loved?

With a groan Sara closed her eyes and whispered, "Heavenly Father, take care of my little girl. Help her to know you love her."

Neddie jerked open the car door and slid under the steering wheel. "What a wind!"

Sara glanced furtively back at the church. "I'm glad I don't have to walk home."

"Sara, is something wrong?"

"I'm all right."

"You can tell me."

"I can't."

"We are friends, you know."

"Please don't ask me, Neddie."

"Is it Roger?"

"Roger?"

"You remember Roger, don't you?" Neddie kept her voice light. She didn't want Sara to guess how she felt about Roger Cairns.

"Everything's fine with Roger. I missed him while I was gone. I hope you kept him company so he didn't get lonely."

Neddie ducked her head to hide the telltale flush as she started her car. "We saw a lot of each other. He missed you." She'd been very careful to keep Roger from guessing how she felt about him. But could she continue to keep it a secret? Her hands trembled on the steering wheel as she pulled out of the parking lot.

How could she fall in love with the man her best friend planned to marry? What would she do after the wedding? Could she spend the rest of her days as a bank teller at Chambers National Bank? Her blond curls would turn gray and her fingers green from counting money.

Sara sat deep in thought and didn't notice that Neddie had suddenly grown very quiet. At the sight of her small white house she sighed in relief. "Thanks, Neddie."

"Want me to come in with you?"

"No thanks. I know you have plans."

"I'm having dinner with Mom and Dad. They'd love to have you come."

Sara shook her head. "Thanks anyway, but I have too much to catch up on after being gone two weeks."

"You get some rest today."

"I'll try." She leaned over and hugged Neddie. "Thanks again. I don't know what I'd do without you."

Neddie flushed and forced a smile. What a hypocrite she was! "See you soon."

A few minutes later Sara stood inside her small living room, her back against the closet where she'd hung her coat and purse. The room was warm but she shivered. Slowly she walked to the loveseat which suited the small room perfectly and sank down on it. Her life was suddenly in turmoil. How could she conduct herself as if nothing unusual had happened?

Suddenly she remembered the autograph party at Roger's Christian Family Bookstore tomorrow. Roger had planned it for several weeks and she couldn't back out now because a ghost from her past had come to haunt her.

"Boyd Allen Collier, I hate you!"

The cruel words filled the air and seemed to blanket the room with darkness. How could she still hate him? It was wrong. She knew Jesus said to love one another. She shook her head. Right now she couldn't deal with that.

Had Boyd seen her at church?

She pulled her knees to her chin and hugged her legs. She knew she looked different, but he'd know her anyway just as she'd known him. If he had seen her, would he have spoken to her? From the day he said he never wanted to see her again he had stayed away as much as possible. If they were forced to be in the same room he ignored her. He probably hated her today as much as he had then.

She moaned and covered her face.

After a long time she clicked on her stereo and changed into jeans and a warm pink sweater. Fixing a cup of tea and a peanut butter and jelly sandwich, Sara sat at the tiny round table in her small kitchen. The yellow and white of the room couldn't cheer her or change the gray, windy day. Budding trees bent with the wind as the music slowly pushed away her agony until she could swallow her food.

Suddenly the phone on her desk rang and she jumped, almost spilling the last of her tea.

"Boyd?" she mouthed.

After the third ring she answered it.

"Hiya, little sister."

She sank to her desk chair. It wasn't Boyd. "Who is this?" she asked sharply.

"George. You know. George Palmer, your oldest brother."

Her hand trembled and she almost dropped the phone. First Boyd and now George! What was happening here? "How'd you find me, George?"

He chuckled. "Were you hiding?"

She hesitated. "No." But she had hoped to stay as far away from her real family as she could.

"I saw a write-up about you in the paper on my way through Chambers, so I thought I'd get in touch with you. I tried yesterday all day."

She licked her dry lips. "I was away."

"I figured." He cleared his throat. "I need some money."

"Go to work like other people."

"Don't be that way, Sara. I thought you being a famous writer and all that you just might want to help me out of a scrape."

"I don't have any money, George. I could give you twenty if that would help."

He laughed a great bark of a laugh. "Twenty? Is that a joke?"

"That's all I can spare, George."

"Then I guess you don't want word of your kid, Carlie."

The strength left her body and she dropped the receiver with a clatter. George's distorted laughter crackled from the phone. The room spun and finally she found the strength to lift the receiver to her ear. "What about Carlie?"

"You ever wonder what became of her?"

"What about her, George?" she cried.

"Ma took her and gave her to a woman who said she'd take good care of her."

"And?"

"She's not doing too good with her."

"Tell me where she is and I'll go get her."

"Give me the money and I'll tell you."

"I told you I don't have any money!"

"Then you won't hear nothing about Carlie from me." He slammed down the receiver and the dial tone buzzed in her ear.

Slowly she dropped the receiver in place. Had George only mentioned Carlie to get money from her? But what if Carlie was unhappy? What if she didn't live in a loving home with caring people?

"My baby," she whispered, rocking back and

forth. Down through the years she'd painted mental pictures of Carlie. Did she have dark brown hair and blue eyes, or light hair and brown eyes like her father?

The phone rang again and Sara scooped it up. "Hello."

"Me again."

"George! Where is Carlie?"

"You ever think about Pete?"

Sara stiffened. "Why?"

"He's out of prison and asking about Carlie."

"Why are you doing this to me, George?"

"I need money," he snapped. "Pete thinks he should know where his kid is and I'm thinking of telling him."

"No!"

"Then give me the money I need."

"That's blackmail, George!"

"So?"

"I don't have any money." Her voice was thick with unshed tears. "I don't, George!"

"Then you get it!"

"But where?"

"I don't know. You probably got rich friends."

She thought of Rita Hardy. "I can't get money for you."

He was quiet a long time. "Sara, do these friends of yours know about your past?"

"George!"

"You get me the money or I tell your story around town. It'll spread like wildfire and you know it, what with you a famous Christian writer and all." He made the word Christian sound like a dirty word.

Her mind whirled. "George, don't do this to me. Please."

"I'll bring Pete here and he might even bring Carlie. A family together at last." George laughed gruffly. "What'd you say, Sara?"

"How much do you need?"

"A million, but five thousand will help."

"How soon?"

"Tomorrow."

"What?" Her voice rose. "How can I get it that fast?"

"That's your problem."

She burst into tears. "George, I can't get it for you. I can't!"

He sighed. "Oh, all right. I'll give you until the end of the week. But that's my final word. You get me that money or, Sara, I will spread your story around and I will tell Pete where he can find you. And Carlie."

She sniffed and blinked back the tears. "I'll get the money for you, George."

* * *

Wind whipping her hair, Amber Ainslie crept around the bushes that led to the back door of the house she'd been staking out for the past three hours. The two men who were to meet her hadn't shown up. Maybe she should go eat lunch and come back later.

She glanced around at the houses on either side

but didn't see any activity there either. Was this a wild goose chase? She pushed her purse strap higher on her shoulder. Jeans hugged her long legs and a yellow sweater and black jacket kept her warm.

She carefully turned the doorknob. To her surprise it wasn't locked and the door opened soundlessly. A chill ran down her spine. Was this a setup? Nobody in his right mind left a door unlocked in this neighborhood.

She eased open the door and stepped inside. Her sneakers were quiet against the linoleum as she crept across the small kitchen. The terrible odor of a dirty bathroom along with stale cigar smoke filled the air. Dirty dishes were stacked in the sink and on the counters. The stove was brown with crusted grease and grime. A mouse streaked across the floor and Amber bit back a scream.

At the doorway she stopped and listened, every fiber of her being tense. Slowly, cautiously she peeked into the room. It was a combination dining and living room. An open door led to a dirty bathroom and another one to an unkempt bedroom. She checked out both but they were empty. Dirty clothes were scattered around the bedroom. One dirty blanket lay in a heap on the bare mattress. The pillow was without a case and looked greasy.

Just then she heard a slight noise from behind a closed door between the bedroom and bathroom. The door was locked with a safety lock. Was someone locked in the closet? She moistened her dry lips with the very tip of her tongue. She waited. Blood pounded in her ears. Slowly she pulled out her revolver and held it ready as she walked across to the locked door.

She eased back the lock, then jerked the door open, her revolver aimed inside. At the sight of a ragged, half-starved boy huddled in a corner she cried out in alarm. The stench almost knocked her off her feet. The boy was too weak to stand. His eyes were glazed over with fear.

"Don't be afraid of me," said Amber softly as she dropped her revolver back in her purse. "I'm going to help you."

"Don't hurt me," he whispered hoarsely.

"I won't. Can you walk? Can you come out to me so we can get you out of here?"

He stared at her a long time and finally pushed himself up and tottered through the mess to her. He was probably about nine years old, but he was so thin and so dirty it was hard to tell.

"I'm going to wrap my jacket around you and take you to my car," she said softly. "I'll take you to the hospital where they'll take care of you."

"Don't hurt me," he whispered.

"I won't. I promise." Carefully she wrapped her jacket around him and picked him up, almost gagging at the smell, then carried him to her car.

* * *

Tears running down her pale cheeks, Carlie huddled deep in the bushes in back of her house. Her muscles were cramped and she was chilled to the bone even though the wind couldn't reach her. Ma and Perkins were still looking for her, still calling her name.

No way would she let Perkins buy her!

She felt a sneeze coming and gritted her teeth, forcing it back.

The dog next door barked. A car honked as it passed, going too fast in a residential area, even a run-down one like this.

A twig poked Carlie in the back. She wanted to move to ease the pain, but she didn't dare.

"Carlie!" shouted Ma, not more than ten feet from where Carlie huddled. "You answer me this minute, little girl, or you're gonna get your tail beat when I do find you!"

Tears burned Carlie's eyes.

"I got candy for you, Carlie," called Perkins.

She'd never take candy from him even if it was a Milky Way, her very favorite candy bar.

After a long time Ma and Perkins walked away. Carlie heard the door slam but she still didn't move. They could be playing a trick on her like she sometimes played on Cindy and Maggie. She'd pretend to run into the house but would only slam the door, then sneak around to hear what they said about her. But they never said much of anything, so she'd go inside for real.

What were Cindy and Maggie doing right now? Maybe dumb old Perkins would want to buy them too. But they lived with their real families, not just a woman called Ma, so he wouldn't be able to buy them.

Carlie groaned. She couldn't stay hidden in the bushes the rest of her life. But where would she go?

Who would help her?

Maybe Maggie would let her stay at her house. She had a bedroom to herself. It was tiny, but it was all hers. Cindy shared a room with two sisters and her new baby brother.

Carlie moved, then froze in place. Ma would look for her at Maggie's and Cindy's houses.

A tear slipped down Carlie's cheek. If she lived in a real home with a real family like she saw on TV she wouldn't have to worry about Perkins buying her. Where was her mom? Her dad? Did they just throw her away because they didn't want her?

With a sob Carlie crept out of the bushes and looked quickly around, then ran to the back of her house. If Ma was off looking for her it would be safe to grab a jacket and a few crackers before she ran away.

She peeked in the two dirty back windows, then ran around to the window she'd climbed out of before. Neither Perkins' car nor Ma's car were in the driveway, so Carlie knew they were gone.

She climbed inside. Smells of coffee and cigarette smoke hung in the air. She slipped on her jacket, grabbed a pack of crackers and a banana and ran to the door to slip out. Just as she reached to turn the knob, Ma pulled into the driveway.

"Oh, no!" cried Carlie, looking around in panic. She couldn't slip out now or Ma would see her.

In a flash she ran to her bedroom and crawled under the bed with the dust balls, lost toys and dirty socks and underwear. The pack of crackers crinkled as she moved and she pushed them away from her. The smell of the banana turned her stomach and she pushed it beside the crackers.

Sweat from fear and from wearing both the sweater and the jacket stung her. Dust tickled her nose and she almost sneezed.

"Forgot my purse," muttered Ma as she walked past Carlie's room to go to hers. "I'll drive all day looking for that girl if I have to. She won't get away from me."

Carlie held her breath and slowly let it out as Ma reached her bedroom. Then she heard Ma walking back, muttering to herself.

"Perkins thinks he can take his money back. Well, he won't have it for long. I'll find that little girl and then I'll get my money back."

Carlie waited until she heard the door slam and Ma drive away, then she slid out, grabbed her crackers and banana, and ran for the door.

Chapter 3

· Amber sank wearily into the chair in the waiting room. The doctor had finally convinced her that the little boy would sleep for hours and didn't need her while he slept. She would have gone back to the house but when she'd called Fritz, he told her to call Deputy Sheriff Grace Donally. Amber had called and the officer who answered said he would contact the Deputy Sheriff immediately.

"She'll listen to you, Red," Fritz had said. "And she will help you if she can. You'll like her, I think. She is as religious as you are."

So Amber waited as patiently as she could for Deputy Sheriff Donally. Someone in a far corner was smoking a cigarette and the terrible smell was wafting through the room. Two girls were playing on the floor, giggling and talking. A man paced the floor. Every time someone walked into the waiting room, Amber expected it to be the deputy sheriff.

A small woman wearing high heels and a beautiful pink dress stepped into the waiting room. She was around thirty with short, light brown hair and keen hazel eyes. "Amber Ainslie?" she asked, glancing around.

Amber jumped up. "Here."

"I'm Grace Donally."

Amber shook hands with her and they sat in a secluded corner. Amber told Grace about the house, the two men she was supposed to meet and about finding the boy. "The doctor said he's been through quite an ordeal. He's dehydrated and hasn't had anything to eat in several days." Amber swallowed hard and bit her lip to keep from bursting into tears. "He's been sexually molested and all he can say is 'Don't hurt me.' Since I was sent to that house on this kiddy porn case I imagine the boy was used for porn photos."

"I'll send a couple of men out to the house immediately." Grace stood up. "And I'll have a look at the boy to see if he's on my list of missing children."

"I'll be on my way while you take care of that. Tell the doctor that I'll be back bright and early tomorrow morning."

"I need to know your source, Amber."

"Sorry. I promised not to reveal my client's identity."

Grace narrowed her eyes. "I hope your client knows he's obstructing justice by not coming to me."

Amber shrugged. She'd had this argument many times before and she didn't want to fight with Grace Donally.

Grace sighed and walked away, her heels tapping the tile.

Amber glanced at her watch. She would call her

client for a long talk, then check to see if the two men had showed up at the house.

* * *

Trembling, Sara punched her mother's phone number. For an hour she had argued with herself about making the call. But fear for Carlie's safety finally gave her the courage. Would Ma speak to her after all this time?

A recording came on to say the number was no longer in use.

Sara dropped the receiver in place, then called information for the number. None was listed. Sara paced her living room wringing her hands. "Why didn't I ask George how I could reach her?"

She could call Mary Collier for Ma's phone number.

"I can't call Mary," whispered Sara. Perspiration dotted her forehead. "But what else can I do?" Carlie was more important than her pride.

Sara scooped up the receiver and punched the buttons that she still remembered after all this time. The phone rang three times and Sara was ready to hang up when someone answered. It was Mary! Just hearing her voice brought tears to Sara's eyes.

Just as Sara was ready to speak she realized Mary's voice was only a recording on an answering machine. At the beep Sara replaced the receiver and turned away with a moan.

"Boyd might know," she said just above a whisper. But how could she reach Boyd?

Once again she picked up the phone and called

information, asking for a listing for Boyd Collier. Her hand trembled as she jotted down Boyd's number. With her last ounce of determination she jabbed his number.

The phone rang and rang and rang but no one answered. Finally Sara hung up, covered her face with her hands and burst into wild tears.

* * *

Carlie stood in front of the elementary school that she attended. A light shone over the wide front doors but the school was dark. This would be a safe place to sleep for the night. She had walked and walked only to find she had walked in a circle since she left Ma's. She had eaten the crackers and the banana, then found an outside water spigot to drink from.

Wind blew her hair in worsening tangles. She shivered and yawned. She was too tired to keep walking.

Maybe she should have gone to the cops. But they might put her in jail. Ma had said you never could trust a cop. She had often said that they tossed bad kids in jail and threw away the key. No, she couldn't go to the cops.

She walked slowly around the brick building. Even in the dark she knew exactly which windows went to her room. Too bad she couldn't open a window and climb inside to sleep.

Finally she crawled between a row of shrubs and the brick building. The ground felt damp, but the wind couldn't reach her and she knew she was completely out of sight. She leaned back against the rough bricks and closed her eyes.

"Momma, where are you?" she whispered.

* * *

Monday morning Sara wearily pushed open the heavy glass door of Christian Family Bookstore. Makeup almost covered the effects of an almost sleepless night. She had tried until two in the morning to reach Mary but got the answering machine every time, so she gave up and tried Boyd without an answer. At last she went to bed. When she finally fell asleep, she'd dreamed of Carlie calling for her.

The warmth of the store wrapped around her and took off the spring chill but couldn't take away the ice around her heart. Could she make it through today and the party Rita Hardy was giving for her tonight? She sighed heavily.

Music filled the room. She opened her purse to drop in her car keys just as she heard a familiar voice—Boyd Collier's. Her purse fell to the floor, scattering the contents. Her face flamed as she scrambled to pick up everything and get away before Boyd saw her. She'd have to forget about the autographing. "Boyd's here!" she mouthed, her eyes wide. Now she could ask him about her family and his and maybe even about Carlie!

Just then Boyd walked around the display shelf. "Need a little help?" He bent to pick up a yellow pencil.

She froze, then slowly stood and faced him with

her chin high and her eyes flashing.

The pencil snapped between his fingers and fell to the floor beside his shiny black shoes. She was absolutely beautiful! "Sara?"

"Hello, Boyd." She forced her voice to stay level. Suddenly she could think of nothing but standing face to face with Boyd Collier.

His dark tie suddenly felt too tight. "It's been a long time."

"Eight years."

"At least." What would she say if she knew that he'd half-heartedly looked for her after she left just to appease his parents? Then, during the last three years, he had looked because he really wanted to find her. His thoughts often turned to her with a longing that he couldn't understand. Each time he angrily pushed them away and continued his life. Here she was standing in front of him looking beautiful and confident and not at all needy or afraid. "How've you been?"

"Just fine. And you?"

He shrugged and grinned. "Can't complain." He looked at her closely, taking in the gray and blue wool coat and skirt with the silky blue blouse. She could easily have stepped out of a fashion magazine. "Mom and Dad wanted to hear from you."

"Yes, well, you made sure that I had to break ties with them." She gathered up the last of her things and pushed them into her purse.

"I'm sorry about that." He scooped up a lipstick and a white ballpoint and held them out to her. She took them and their hands brushed. A shock passed through him and her pulse leaped with awareness.

Suddenly she remembered Carlie and George. She took an unsteady breath. "I tried to call my ma yesterday."

"They moved away from Green Lake last year, but I don't know where they went."

"Oh!" Sara bit her lower lip. "I also tried to call your mother."

"They're away on vacation. But they would've been glad to hear from you."

Sudden tears pricked her eyes and she turned just as Roger Cairns strode from the back room toward her. "Roger!" She hurried to meet him. He was just a little taller than she and he wore a navy suit with a red tie. His brown hair was cut short and parted on the left side. His dark eyes crinkled as he smiled.

"Sara!" He caught her close in a warm hug, then let her go. "I missed you!"

She glanced at Boyd in time to see his frown and she flushed. She forced her mind off Carlie for the moment. "Roger Cairns, Boyd Collier. Roger owns this bookstore." Could Roger feel her tremble?

"We've met," said Roger with a laugh. "We have a wonderful surprise for you, Sara."

"Wonderful surprise," said Boyd with a sudden twinkle in his eyes that alarmed her.

"What is it?" she asked.

Roger felt the tension in the air, but couldn't understand it. "Boyd is going to autograph books today with you."

She stepped back. "What?"

Boyd laughed. "Are you surprised that I write,

or that I'm taking part of your limelight today?"

She stood very still. "My limelight?" Did he know who she was?

"I learned that you're the famous Sara Noreen, writer of wonderful fiction for children."

His praise pleased her more than she cared to admit. "I'm surprised you know that."

"Not as surprised as I was when I found out. Who would have thought you'd become a writer?"

"Do you two know each other?" asked Roger in surprise.

Boyd nodded and Sara shot him a warning look. "We go back a long way," said Boyd.

"I know his family," said Sara weakly.

Roger moved restlessly. "Boyd stopped in while you were gone and said he was free to come today to autograph. It gave me enough time to advertise."

Sara gripped her purse tightly. What was Boyd planning? Would he find pleasure in telling her readers and Roger all about her terrible past?

Boyd saw her sudden fear and smiled, trying to reassure her.

The door opened and the bell tinkled. "Here comes a customer. Boyd, take Sara to the table that I showed you. I have name tags for you both and piles of books on the table." Roger smiled, unsure if he wanted to leave Sara alone with Boyd. Something was going on between the two of them that he didn't like. Sara's secretive attitude about her past had always bothered him. "I'll be over to talk to you when I can."

Sara watched Roger walk to the customer and

greet him pleasantly. Roger was kind-hearted and Sara liked that quality in him. Finally she turned to Boyd and said stiffly, "Show me the table."

"Follow me." He touched her arm. She jerked away from him and he frowned. Maybe he shouldn't have come to sign autographs with her today.

At the table he took her coat and hung it in the closet. Slowly he walked back to her. "Are you still upset with me, Sara?"

"Shouldn't I be?"

"Yes, well, maybe you should. I said a lot of things to you that I've regretted."

She pressed the name tag against her jacket with a trembling hand. "Do you know where my baby, Carlie, is?"

"No. Should I?"

"I have to make sure she's all right."

He lifted a dark brow. "Why now, after all this time?"

"We'd better talk about this later." She glanced at Roger. Boyd saw her look and frowned.

"I didn't know you and Roger were *that* friendly," he said.

"We're practically engaged."

His stomach tightened and he dropped to his chair. "That is a surprise. He didn't tell me."

"Why should he?"

"You're right." Boyd breathed in the delicate fragrance of her perfume as she sat beside him. Should he tell her the real reason he was here? He knew he couldn't, not now anyway. He cleared his throat. "You didn't seem surprised to see me here."

"Did you think I'd fall into your arms?" she asked coldly.

"There is always hope," he said lightly. He had wanted to surprise her and get her true reaction to him. Maybe her true reaction was that she didn't care if he was here or a million miles away. Had he really expected her to remain the same girl who had declared undying love for him? He sighed heavily and said again, "There is always hope."

She turned away from him in confusion. What could he mean?

He fingered his ballpoint and stared down at his pile of books. Now that he'd seen her, maybe he could get on with his life. Each time he'd been close to falling in love, Sara's face had come between him and the woman. When he'd prayed for his wife, her face had appeared. At first he thought it was because he needed to ask her forgiveness for hurting her. Later he wondered if her love for him was as strong as she had declared it was. Now that Sara was practically engaged and doing fine without the Colliers, he could get on with his life. He would apologize for the terrible things he had said to her and never have to see her again. He nodded. Joyln was hoping they'd get serious. Maybe now they could

"Here come our first fans," whispered Sara as two girls walked toward the table. Sara had autographed books many times before, but it never ceased to thrill her. Today she knew she could keep her mind off George and Carlie and on the job at hand.

The red-headed girl smiled at Boyd, then turned to Sara. "We love your books." She picked up the second book in the series. "I want this one."

Smiling, Sara took it. "What's your name?"

"I'm Lisa and she's Gale."

Sara signed with a flourish, glad that Boyd was sitting beside her to watch how well-known she'd become. She was no longer the foster girl with nothing of her own, not even a good name.

"I read your first book three times," said Gale. "It is my very, very, very favorite book in the whole world!"

"Thank you." Sara wanted to peek at Boyd to see his reaction, but she continued her conversation with the girls.

Several people lined up for Boyd's autograph, talking to him and asking him questions. Sara tried to listen, but too many people came for her autograph.

During a lull Roger sat on the edge of the table next to Sara and took her hand. "You both are a hit with my customers."

Boyd's smile froze in place as he watched Roger lean over and kiss Sara. Were they really in love? Did she love Roger as much as she'd loved him?

"I have a couple of errands to run," said Roger. "Lucy will be at the checkout counter if you need anything before I get back."

Sara silently watched him walk out the door.

"So, you two are going to get married?" Boyd tried to find satisfaction in the thought, but he couldn't. "When?"

"We haven't made it official yet," Sara answered stiffly. "Maybe by the end of the year."

Just then the bell over the door tinkled and Sara looked up to see George step inside. The color drained from her face and she clutched Boyd's arm.

He glanced at her hand on his arm, then raised his eyes to her pale cheeks. He turned to see who she was staring at. "Who is it?" he asked in a low, tight voice.

"George. My brother."

"Why does he frighten you?"

"No one here knows about my past."

"And do you think he will tell?"

"Yes. If he gets the chance. I don't want Roger to know about me."

"If he really loves you he won't care about your past."

"How can you say that?"

"Why?"

She narrowed her eyes. "If I would have been one of your well-brought-up girlfriends, maybe you would have returned my love."

Tension crackled between them. "Maybe you're right."

George spotted them and strode back to the table. Laugh lines spread from his frosty blue eyes to his mussed brown hair. Day-old whiskers covered his face and neck. He wore a stained blue jacket, a plaid shirt and jeans. "What'd you know. My little sister really is an author. And Boyd Collier beside her. Well, well."

"Don't make trouble, George," whispered Sara.

"Hey, I came to buy me a book," he said with a loud laugh.

Boyd pushed himself up. "How are you, George?"

"I could be better." He bent down to Sara. "You know what I mean?"

She nodded, her heart thudding painfully against her ribcage.

"Just what is it you want from Sara, George?" asked Boyd.

George turned cold eyes on Boyd. "It's none of your business. This is between me an' her."

"Don't cause a scene, George," said Sara, just above a hoarse whisper. She wanted to ask him about Carlie, but knew he wouldn't tell her anything.

He flung out his arms. "Me cause a scene? I came to buy a book. I didn't know a Palmer had this many words in 'em. The ones we do know couldn't be printed in here." He slapped the book on his palm. "You must've learned all this from living with the Colliers."

"Where do you live, George?" Boyd walked around the table and leaned against it beside George.

"Grand Rapids, but I see Ma and Roy regular."

Sara's heart leaped. "Where do they live?"

"They just moved again, so I don't know."

Sara bit back a moan of despair.

George shook the book at Boyd. "I even run across your folks. They haven't been the same since they took this one in." He tapped Sara's arm and she jerked away from him. He scowled. "I'll be in touch."

Abruptly he strode away to pay for the book. It seemed funny to think of his sister as religious. Nobody else had been in their family. Once he'd dated a girl who tried to get him to go to church with her but when he wouldn't, she'd dropped him flat.

He paid for the book and walked outside into the brisk wind. He might give the book to Ma so she could see how Sara had turned out. It would make her happy. She was always asking about Sara. George rolled his eyes. "As if she cares about any of us." He slid into his beat-up Chevy and drove away. Once he got that money from Sara, he'd drive right out of the state and never return.

Inside the store, Sara signed more books while Boyd talked with several people. She was glad George had left before the swarm of customers walked in and saw him.

When they were alone again Boyd said, "Does he want money?"

She hesitated, then nodded. "Or he'll tell everyone about my past."

"Don't give it to him. If you do, he'll blackmail you the rest of your life."

She sagged in her chair. She hadn't thought of that.

"Let me take care of George."

"How?"

"I'll tell him that if he doesn't leave you alone, I'll report him to the police. With his record he can't afford that."

She gripped his arm. "I can't let you do that."

"Why?"

"He said . . . said he'd tell Pete where I am. And where Carlie is."

"Pete?"

She locked her icy hands in her lap. "Carlie's dad."

"Oh."

"Pete is out of prison now. I don't want to see him and I don't want him near Carlie."

"How can I help?"

"George wants five thousand dollars before the end of this week."

Boyd sat quietly a long time. "I'll pay him."

Sara gasped, her eyes wide. "Would you really do that for me?"

"Sure. I owe you something. Don't you think?"

"That was a long time ago."

"I know. And I've been sorry for all the terrible things I said to you ever since."

"You have?"

He nodded.

She couldn't imagine him being sorry. She didn't know what to say. Her eyes locked with his and she couldn't look away.

"I've been invited to Rita Hardy's party tonight," he said.

"Oh."

"Do you mind?"

"Should I?"

He smiled. "How is it that you became a writer, Sara?"

She shrugged. It was much easier to talk about writing than about her past. "I took another class in creative writing after I left high school and I liked it. I had a daytime job as a typist and went to night class. I sold a short story and I was hooked. How about you? I thought you were going to be a history teacher."

He laughed softly. "I'd forgotten that. I guess after reading all those books on self-improvement and listening to speakers and tapes, I realized that I had something to say too. I talked to a lot of people and wrote down their experiences. I knew I wanted to write a book showing that with Christ as the true answer, we can accomplish anything that we want. So, here I am. And here you are."

"I never expected to see you again."

"I'm sure you never wanted to after our last meeting."

Color stained her cheeks. "I was very young."

"And so was I."

She saw the pain in his eyes and she nodded. He *was* sorry, but she might not be able to forgive or forget that easily. She turned away from Boyd to see Roger watching them. She flushed and tried to smile.

Chapter 4

Amber paced the study while she waited for her client. The two men never had showed up yesterday and she needed answers. She'd hit a dead end and she didn't like that at all. She flipped back her long, fiery-red hair, then tucked her blue blouse into her dress slacks. Later she'd call Mina to see if she had learned anything new. She grinned as she thought of Mina Streeby. That woman knew everything about everything. Since her husband died, Mina had used all her time and energy to learn things she always wanted to know. She was Amber's land-lady and she also did a lot of the footwork for Ainslie Detective Agency cases. She was even trying to find Amber just the right country home.

Just then Amber's client walked in. She was in her forties, medium weight, hair dyed light brown and a serious, almost frightened, look on her face.

"I'm sorry to keep you waiting, Amber."

"Mrs. Sawyer, we must talk."

"My husband is gone so we are free to talk. Would you like a cup of tea or anything?"

"No. Thanks." Amber brushed a strand of red hair away from her face. "I thought you were going to tell Pastor Sawyer that you spoke with me."

Midge Sawyer wrung her hands and shook her head. "I just couldn't tell him! I was hoping everything would get resolved so I wouldn't have to."

She looked ready to cry. Amber led her to the leather couch and sat with her. "Surely your husband would understand."

"No. I don't think he would. He protects the people he counsels."

"Even when it will hurt someone else?" asked Amber softly.

A tear slipped down Midge's round cheek. "Maybe it's me I'm trying to protect."

"How is that?"

"I overheard another conversation of Mrs. Drift's that Ted knows nothing about. It happened just after he left her hospital room." Midge nervously rubbed her gray skirt over her knees. "When I stepped into the room the curtain around Mrs. Drift was closed and they didn't know I was there. I sat quietly in a corner behind another curtain, planning to leave when Ted did. But when I heard what they said I didn't want Ted to know that I'd heard, so I stayed until I thought he'd be gone. I was ready to slip out without being seen and then she made the call. I waited to listen. But I do hate to be considered an eavesdropper!"

Amber forced herself to stay calm. She wanted to tell Midge Sawyer to forget her feelings for a minute and think about the danger to everyone involved with kiddy porn. "Mrs. Sawyer. Midge. Please, talk to me. It's a matter of life and death. I found one of the missing boys who was probably used for porn photos or videos. He was almost dead." She told about going to the house and finding the boy. "I checked with the hospital just before I came here. The doctor said the boy would live but it would take a miracle for him to lead a normal life."

Midge dabbed her eyes with the corner of a white hanky.

"You told me about the house. You said there were two men who would talk to me and give me information."

Midge nodded. "I knew the boy was there," she whispered. "Mrs. Drift said so on the phone to someone."

Amber stiffened. "Who was she speaking to?"

"I don't know. Honestly, I don't. But I thought the men would be there. The men were in charge of the kids."

Amber could barely breathe. "Kids?"

"The ones they used in their last porn video. Mrs. Drift said so. She told my husband that she suspected something terrible was going on in the house next door to her. But she only hinted at things." Midge rubbed her cheeks and sniffed. "He didn't know I heard, then later I overheard Mrs. Drift make a phone call. I know I shouldn't have listened, but I had this terrible feeling that something worse than I could imagine was going on. I was right."

"So where are the other children?"

"I don't know! If I did, I'd tell you. I want you to find them."

"I must speak with Mrs. Drift. How can I reach her?"

"I don't know. She said she was moving out of state as soon as she was released from the hospital." Midge bit her lip and looked helplessly at Amber. "I'm afraid I...I made sure she was gone before I talked to you so that you couldn't interrogate her."

Amber leaped up, her temper flaring. "If I'd known about this soon enough, maybe all the kids would be free today!"

Midge burst into tears. "I know and I'm *so* sorry!"

Amber forced back her anger and patted Midge on the back. "I know you are. Maybe there's something you haven't told me that would help. Please go over your husband's conversation again as well as Mrs Drift's phone call."

* * *

Boyd held Sara's coat for her while Roger closed out the cash register for the day. "I'll get the money for George to you as soon as I can," he said in low voice for her ears alone.

"I shouldn't take it." She looked helplessly at him. "But I must. Unless there's a way out that I can't see right now."

"We'll be praying that God shows you a way out."

She nodded. "Thank you." She slipped into her coat and picked up her purse. Autographing had gone well and most of the time she was able to keep her mind on it. "Boyd, I will pay back every penny."

"Don't even think about it now. I want to help you. I'm still not giving up the idea of talking to George. Maybe I can get him to tell me where Carlie is."

"I feel so overwhelmed right now."

He smiled and tapped the tip of her nose. "Aren't you glad we don't live by feelings? We live by faith. Faith can move mountains. And George looks like a mighty big mountain right now. Together with God's help we will succeed."

His words warmed her heart and gave her hope. For one wild moment she wanted to lean against him and have him hold her.

"I'll see you later at the Hardy's," he said softly.

"Later," she whispered.

* * *

Carlie peeked out from behind the couch in the teachers' lounge. She'd sneaked into school when the doors opened this morning and had stayed hidden all day. At lunch she managed to grab food without being seen. Finally the building was empty and she could walk around freely. Why, she could probably live in the school until she was eighteen and on her own! There was food, a warm place to sleep and restrooms. She rubbed a hand over her dirty jeans and sweater. She would look for a change of clothes in the Lost and Found box.

A floor creaked and she jumped in fright. She patted her racing heart and whispered, "It wasn't nothin' at all."

She walked down the hall. It was strange being the only person in the entire building. Her face puckered and she whimpered.

Would she have to stay hidden until she was eighteen or could she find help somewhere? Once today she'd heard Maggie and Cindy talking about her. She wanted to let them know that she was safe but she couldn't without disclosing her hiding place. Besides, they might tell Ma. And Ma would tell Perkins.

Carlie walked back into the teachers' lounge and dropped down on the couch. "No way will Perkins buy me!"

* * *

Roger stood just inside the door of Sara's house and took her in his arms. "What's wrong, Sara? You've been very quiet since we left the bookstore. You hardly spoke at dinner."

She sighed tiredly. "I'm sorry, Roger. I wish Rita would excuse me from the party tonight so we could have time to talk."

"But it's in your honor." He kissed her. "I'd like to have time alone with you, too. I missed you a lot the past two weeks."

"And I missed you!" How she wished she was safely married to him so that Boyd's entrance into her life couldn't change anything. Or George's. Also she felt guilty about the emotions that Boyd had stirred in her. Oh, she must put her guard up! It wouldn't do to fall in love with him again. She moved restlessly in Roger's arms and he released her with a slight frown.

"Can't you tell me what's bothering you, Sara? You know I'll help any way I can."

"I know you would, but I can't talk about it yet." She pushed her long hair back. "Sit down and relax while I go change for the party."

He sat on the loveseat and leaned his head back while she ran to her bedroom. Suddenly he remembered that he'd promised to give Neddie a ride to the party tonight. He glanced at his watch. She was probably wondering where he was. He thought about phoning her, but Sara rushed in and said she was ready. He jumped up. "I forgot to tell you that we're picking Neddie up."

"Oh?"

"You don't mind, do you?"

"Of course not." She grabbed her coat and purse. "Let's go." How could she even think about going to a party when her life was in such turmoil? She bit back a tired sigh.

A few minutes later Roger drove to Neddie's and ran up the walk to get her. Sara leaned her head back and closed her eyes. Why had she ever agreed to let Rita have a party for her? But then, when they'd planned it, her life had been wonderful.

Neddie greeted Roger stiffly while her heart raced just being near him. She should have refused his offer to pick her up, but her car was in the shop and she didn't want to stay home from Sara's party. It wouldn't be right.

"Is something wrong, Neddie?" asked Roger softly. He couldn't understand his feelings for

Neddie, but he knew that he liked seeing a smile on her face.

"I hate to be in the way."

Roger stopped at the curb and frowned at Neddie. The streetlights shone down on her. "Why are you talking that way? You're never in the way!"

She smiled slightly. "Thanks."

He opened the back door and she slipped inside with a quiet hello to Sara.

Sara glanced back with a smile. "Hi, Neddie. How was your day?"

"The same as usual. What can be different in a bank?"

Roger chuckled as he pulled away from the curb. "A robbery."

Neddie laughed. "You're right about that."

Sara's stomach knotted. With George in town a bank robbery wasn't a joke.

A few minutes later Roger parked the car along the street behind a blue Olds and they walked to the Hardy's front door. Cool wind blew Sara's hair away from her face. The soft light from the front porch glowed invitingly. Roger rang the doorbell and the door swung open. Both Bob and Rita Hardy stood there, smiling as they ushered them in. The Hardys were middle-aged, wealthy, nice looking and, much to Rita's sorrow, childless.

"Now the party can begin," said Rita, giving Sara a warm hug.

Sara glanced quickly around. She spotted Boyd as he stepped through a double door. He wore a black suit with a crisp white shirt and red tie that was far from conservative. Her heart lurched and she reached back for Roger's hand only to find that he'd walked away with Bob and Neddie. Rita turned to greet other guests and Sara was forced to face Boyd alone.

"Hello," she said through her dry throat.

He smiled. "You look beautiful, Sara."

She flushed. "Thank you." Had she dressed in blue because it was his favorite color? Abruptly she pushed the thought aside.

"I have someone I want you to meet."

"Oh?"

"She's standing over there talking to the pastor and his wife."

"The redhead?"

"Yes. And she just might be our answer to prayer." Boyd started across the room with Sara and smiled as the redhead turned and walked away from the Sawyers. She was tall and slender with a mass of brilliant red hair and a gorgeous smile. She wore a pink dress that looked fantastic with her red hair. "Sara Palmer, Amber Ainslie," said Boyd. "The party is in Sara's honor, Amber. She's a writer. Juvenile fiction read by kids all over the world."

Amber held out her hand and Sara shook it. "I'm glad to meet you, Sara," said Amber.

"Are you a writer too?" asked Sara.

Amber chuckled. "I'm a private investigator."

Sara's eyes widened. Maybe Amber *was* an answer to her prayers. When she finally had a chance to speak to Amber alone she said in a low, tight voice, "I need your help. Here's my card. Could you come see me early in the morning? It's very important. Urgent, in fact."

Amber saw Sara's quiet desperation and nodded as she stuck the card in her purse. Thoughtfully she watched Sara walk away to speak to Rita Hardy.

Just then Amber spotted Deputy Sheriff Grace Donally. She was dressed in black and red and looked more like a successful businesswoman than a deputy sheriff. Amber walked to her side and greeted her with a smile. "Business or pleasure tonight, Grace?"

Grace smiled and shrugged. "A little of both actually. Pastor Sawyer knows I've been trying to break the kiddy porn ring and he told me that someone from this house was involved."

Amber's eyes widened. She'd learned that Mrs. Drift had called someone at the Hardys from the hospital. The Hardys had a big staff. "I didn't realize Pastor Sawyer was helping you with this."

Grace nodded. "He is against pornography and is doing everything he can to stamp it out."

Amber glanced at the Sawyers, then back at Grace. "Does his wife know it?"

Grace shook her head. "He doesn't want her to know because she gets frightened too easily. He doesn't want to do anything to upset her."

Amber bit back a grin. Those two needed to communicate better. "Have you learned who from here is involved?"

"No. That's why I'm speaking to you about it. With both of us working carefully so as not to arouse suspicion maybe we can learn the truth quicker. I didn't want to bring in any of my people. I'm here as a guest. I know most of these people. How is it you were invited?"

"I heard about the party and asked that I get an invitation." She didn't want to tell Grace that Midge Sawyer had called Rita Hardy for the invitation. "So, here I am. I've asked a few questions of the staff, but hopefully nothing that would arouse suspicion."

"I've spoken to the kitchen staff. But nothing so far."

"So did I. What about Bob and Rita Hardy?" asked Amber as she looked at the couple across the room where they were laughing and talking to the Sawyers.

Grace sighed. "I hate to think it could be either of them. They're model citizens. He has a fine real estate business and she does charity work. Right now she's collecting money for a burn center at the hospital. Sara Palmer is her secretary."

"Does Rita have an office here?"

"Yes."

Amber narrowed her eyes. "So that means Sara is in this house at times."

"Yes"

"Just what do you know about Sara Palmer?" asked Amber.

"She's lived here for four years and is a wonderful person. I know nothing of her life before that. I've read her books and enjoy them. She seems to be a dedicated Christian."

Amber fingered her necklace thoughtfully.

A few minutes later Rita Hardy motioned for Sara to join her. Sara excused herself to Roger and hurried after Rita. They stopped in Rita's study where they usually worked together. Rita seemed very nervous.

"Sara, who is Amber Ainslie?"

Sara lifted a fine brow questioningly. "Didn't you invite her tonight?"

"Yes. But I don't know if we should trust her."

Weakly Sara leaned back against the desk. "Why do you say that?"

"She's making Bob very nervous. And I learned that she was asking my kitchen staff questions."

"She is a private investigator. Maybe she's working on a case."

Rita trembled. "Here? In my home?"

Sara smiled. "Maybe she was asking for a recipe."

"Has she questioned you?"

"No. Well, she did ask about my work, but that's only normal."

"She asked me about mine, too. But as you say, that's only normal." Absently Rita rubbed her hand up and down the sleeve of her mauve dress. "I hope she doesn't think something underhanded is going on with the way we're collecting money for the burn center."

"I'm sure she doesn't. Nothing *is* wrong."

"You're right." Rita seemed to relax. "If you learn anything, will you let me know?"

"Of course. But there's probably nothing to

learn." Sara thought about her own dark secrets and wondered if others could be hiding secrets just as terrible or maybe even worse.

Rita walked to the door, then turned to Sara again. "I want you to take tomorrow off, Sara. I'm sure you need a rest."

"Thank you. I do."

Later Sara slipped her hand through Roger's arm and leaned her forehead against his wool jacket. The group around them talked about the burn center that would be built next year at Mercy Hospital if Rita Hardy could raise enough money for it. Sara caught Boyd's eye from across the room. She flipped back her hair and kept a firm hold on Roger. Boyd finally turned away and spoke to Neddie beside the piano.

Sara knew that several of the guests had already left. Her feet ached and it was hard to keep a smile on her face.

Roger leaned down to her. "Ready to go yet?"

"Yes." She glanced at Neddie. "I hope Neddie won't mind."

Roger frowned. "She's been spending too much time with Boyd tonight. I hope he's not leading her on."

"I'm sure she can take care of herself."

"Not with a man like Boyd. I noticed today what a charmer he is." Roger walked purposefully toward Neddie and Boyd, and Sara was forced to follow.

"I was just talking about leaving," said Neddie with a laugh. Her hazel eyes sparkled and her face glowed.

Her face set, Sara shot a look at Boyd. He looked questioningly down his long nose at her.

Roger rested a hand on Neddie's shoulder. "We're leaving now if that's all right with you."

"I'll take her home," said Boyd.

"No!" Roger shook his head and Sara looked at him in surprise. "We brought her, so I think we should take her home."

"She can do as she pleases," said Boyd. "Neddie, may I drive you home?"

Sara wanted to grab Neddie and pull her away from Boyd, but she kept her hands at her sides and a smile glued to her face.

Roger frowned and gruffly said goodnight to them and to the Hardys. Sara waved at Amber Ainslie, wondering if she made a mistake in asking Amber for help. Surely doing something was better than doing nothing at all. She walked to the car with Roger.

"I don't understand Neddie at all," said Roger as he drove away from the Hardys. "She's completely taken in by Boyd Collier."

"I noticed." Sara leaned back and locked her hands over her purse. What was Boyd up to? Would he break Neddie's heart as he had hers?

"She's usually so level-headed."

"I know."

"I think I'll have a talk with her. Maybe I'll see her tomorrow or call her later tonight."

Sara shot a questioning look at him, but he was too deep in thought to notice.

Several minutes later Roger stopped outside

Sara's house. He'd been very quiet, thinking of Neddie and her attraction for Boyd. Roger couldn't understand his anger or his jealousy. Why should it bother him for Neddie to be attracted to Boyd?

"See you tomorrow, Roger," said Sara softly.

He leaned over and absently kissed her cheek. "Tomorrow."

Her mind churned with things she wanted to say to Amber Ainslie when she came in the morning.

Chapter 5

Dressed in jeans and a pink sweater, Sara looked out her window at the morning sun shining on the dew-bright grass. A robin hopped across the lawn. A car drove past. Listlessly Sara walked to her tiny kitchen. Would Amber Ainslie really come? And if she did, would she help her find Carlie? Could she help get George out of her life?

At eight-thirty Amber knocked on the door. Sara flung it open in relief. "I'm so glad you came!"

As Amber draped her jacket over a chair she could see the strain in Sara's face. Amber wore new jeans and a bright green sweater. Matching green combs held back her fiery red hair. "How can I help you, Sara?"

Sara took a deep breath and plunged right into her story, every terrible detail. "So I need someone to find Carlie before something awful happens to her."

"Would your brother do something to physically harm Carlie?"

"I don't think so. But I read in last night's paper about kiddy porn showing up around here. He is desperate for money and he might hand her over to the ones involved in it. He did deal in adult porn, so maybe he does the other too." Sara shuddered.

Excitement surged inside Amber, but she didn't let it show. Maybe she was getting somewhere after all. Last night she had finally learned to whom Mrs. Drift had spoken at the Hardy house only to find that the woman, Olga Swensen, was not available. Sharing the information with Grace was helpful because Grace would immediately try to find Olga Swensen. Things were finally falling into place.

Amber studied Sara. "Do you have any idea where Carlie is?"

"No. But George knows and so does my mother."

"But you don't know where your mother is."

"No."

"And Pete?" Amber pulled a notebook out of her purse jotting down names and information to jog her memory later.

"I don't know where he is. I haven't seen him for ten years—since just after Carlie was born."

"You say he was in prison for dealing drugs. Did he have any connection with porn?"

"I have no idea."

"Describe George to me so that I can find him." Mina was working on the computer to find information about George and Pete as well as Sara's parents. "Since he's passing through town he would probably be staying in a motel, wouldn't he?"

"I don't know. He didn't mention that he knew anyone in town." Sara described George and the car he was driving outside Roger's bookstore. "I don't want to give George the money, but I can't let anything bad happen to my little girl."

"He gave you until the end of the week so let me work on it. Just hang in there until you hear from me." Amber dropped the notebook back in her purse, slipped on her jacket and walked to the door. "I'll be praying for you."

"Thank you! And for Carlie too."

Amber nodded. "For Carlie too."

Minutes after Amber drove away someone knocked on Sara's door. She peeked out and, to her surprise, found Boyd standing there. His sable brown hair was wind-blown and his eyes were thoughtful. "Good morning," she said, suddenly breathless. He smelled of fresh air and aftershave.

"We have to talk," he said.

"About the money?" Her hands trembled as she took his jacket and hung it in the closet. She pulled her sweater down over her jeans and nervously pushed her hair back. "I don't blame you if you decided not to help me."

"It's not the money. I'll have it for you tomorrow."

"Oh." She told him about speaking with Amber and that she wouldn't need the money so soon.

"Hiring her was a good idea, Sara. She seems to be a lady who gets what she goes after."

"Unlike me," Sara said under her breath.

"Let's sit down," he said, motioning to the loveseat.

Her nerves were jangled. Suddenly she felt

awkward and sixteen again. "I'll stand."

"Have it your way." He stabbed his long fingers through his hair, then smoothed it in place. "I don't know where to begin."

"Then don't start. Let's talk about last night with Neddie."

"Funny you should mention her. I think I'll start there. But first let's sit down. I'd hate to see you fall on the floor in a dead heap." He waited and his face softened. "Please, Sara. Sit down and listen to me. It's important."

She eased her way around the chair and sank into the cushioned softness while he sat on the loveseat. She locked her icy hands in her lap. "Well?"

"Don't look so scared, honey."

She lifted her chin. "Don't call me honey!"

He crossed his long legs and rubbed a hand over the soft denim of his jeans as he looked around. "I like your place."

"You didn't come to talk about my home."

"No. I didn't."

She moved restlessly. The room suddenly seemed small and confining.

"I can see it's hard for you to be alone with me."

"You saw to that years ago," she said bitterly.

He rubbed an unsteady hand across his jaw. "I know and I'm sorry. Can you forgive me?"

"I can't erase the words you said. I will never forget the words or the pain!"

He leaned toward her and she stiffened. "Sara, I am very sorry for what I did to you. I was young. And frightened."

"Frightened?"

"You made me feel things that I'd never felt before."

She pressed her hands to her fiery cheeks. "Oh, how could I ever think that I loved you, or wanted you!"

He sucked in air. "Maybe you didn't love me."

Her eyes flashed. "You'd like to think that, wouldn't you? You had such a low opinion of me. But I did love you. How stupid of me!"

"And now you think you're in love with Roger Cairns."

"I do love him!"

"Have you noticed that your friend, Neddie, is miserable?"

Sara frowned. "I have noticed. But what is that to you?"

"Neddie is in love."

Sara stiffened. "With you? That's fast work."

Boyd frowned. "Neddie is deeply in love with Roger Cairns."

"What?" cried Sara.

"It's true love, Sara. Not the pitiful little feeling you have for him that you call love."

Sara grabbed a throw pillow and hugged it to herself. "What do you know about my feelings?"

"I've seen the two of you together. I've watched you. There's no spark, no magic."

"Oh, what do you know about it?" Her eyes flashed. "You can't recognize love when you see it!"

"You're probably right, Sara. Now, let's get

back to Neddie. What are you going to do?"

Sara tucked her chestnut-brown hair behind her ears. "Do you think just because you're loaning me money that you can presume to tell me how to run my life?"

"It has nothing to do with the money. I want you to be happy."

"I am happy! And so is Roger!"

"Roger can't see past you to know that Neddie loves him. You're a beautiful, desirable, mysterious woman. Neddie is sweet and cute and he's known her for years."

"What are you suggesting?"

Boyd leaned back with a grin. A passing car honked. "That you dump Roger."

Sara stared in shock at Boyd. "I can't. I won't."

"I told Neddie that you didn't really love Roger and that she should take him away from you."

She leaped up, her fists doubled at her sides. "You can't be serious!"

"That's what she said. She loves you and wouldn't do anything to hurt you." He stood up and faced her. "But you're hurting her, Sara."

"And you're hurting me."

"Not on purpose."

"I think you are. I think you wanted to find a way to interfere in my life, so you did it this way." She walked to the door. "Go home and leave me alone."

Boyd stood before her, an earnest look on his face. "Sara, I don't want to hurt you. I want only the best for you and I don't think Roger is the best for you. Look in your heart. Do you love him the way you loved me?"

"I don't have the same passion now that I had then. How could I love him as much?"

"I'm sure you've prayed that the Lord would help you know if Roger is the right man for you."

"Boyd, I'm all grown up now. It's not necessary for you to guide my life the way you did years ago."

He grinned. "You're right, of course. I'm sorry. But I do want the very best for you. I mean it." Was it possible that he had loved her years ago and that the love still burned in his heart? The thought wiped the grin off his face.

She could tell he was serious and it pleased her.

Suddenly the phone rang and she jumped. Boyd caught her icy hand in his. She clung to him, her eyes glued to the phone.

"Would you like me to answer it?"

"No. I'll get it." She pulled free and walked to the phone. It helped to have Boyd stay at her side as she picked up the receiver. "Hello," she said.

"Who've you been talking to about me, dear sister?"

"George?" She reached for Boyd's hand and gripped it.

"Of course it's me. Now, tell me who you talked to about me."

"Why?"

"The police questioned me, that's why!"

Her throat closed over. "About what?"

"Kiddy porn! Can you believe it? And I don't have nothing to do with that!"

"I didn't talk to the police about you, George. They probably questioned anyone in town with a prison record."

"You might be right." He cleared his throat. "It's not safe for me to stay in Chambers. I can't wait around until the end of the week. I need the money now, Sara."

She looked helplessly at Boyd. "You need the money now?"

"Let me have the phone," whispered Boyd, but she shook her head and wouldn't let him take it. He leaned his head down by hers so he could hear George.

"You get the money to me or I just might hand Carlie over to the kiddy porn ring."

Fear pricked her skin. "You wouldn't do that!"

"I would!"

"You said you don't have anything to do with kiddy porn."

"But Pete does. And he's still mad at you for not having an abortion after he had it all set up. I'll hand Carlie over to him. That's a sure enough promise, Sara."

She knew he meant it. Weakly she sagged against Boyd. "I'll have the money tomorrow just after the bank opens."

"I'll pick it up at your place at nine-thirty sharp." He hung up with a bang.

Boyd took the receiver from her trembling hand and set it in place. He turned her to him and held her close.

"I must find Carlie," said Sara with a sob.

"I'll try to reach Amber Ainslie and tell her what George said. I heard her say she was staying at the Holiday Inn." He called the Inn and when he learned Amber was out, he left a message for her to call Sara immediately.

"Thank you, Boyd." She dabbed tears away. "Is there any way to reach your mother to ask her about Carlie?"

"No. They said they were going to stay far away from telephones during this vacation."

Sara sighed a long ragged sigh.

"I'm going to stay here with you until Amber calls," said Boyd.

"I'm glad. I couldn't handle being alone right now. Would you like a cup of tea?"

"Yes. Yes, I would." He wanted to pull her close again, but knew he didn't dare.

Sara led him to the kitchen where she put the kettle on to boil. Silently she prayed for Carlie.

Boyd watched Sara as she fixed the tea. He realized he would need to be absolutely honest with her to be fair to her. It was not right to put off the truth any longer. He waited until their tea was finished.

"I have something important to tell you, Sara," he said in a low, tight voice.

Her heart lurched, then thudded on. Suddenly her sweater felt too hot.

"Don't look so frightened."

"But you sound so serious!"

He paced the small kitchen, then sat down again looking at her as if he couldn't get enough of her.

Her heart pounded until it was a loud hammering in her ears.

"You're so beautiful," he whispered hoarsely.

She moistened her dry lips with the tip of her tongue. Butterflies fluttered in her stomach. "Maybe you'd better leave," she whispered.

"I can't." He leaned toward her. "I've waited too long. I've searched too long."

"What...what do you mean?"

"After all these years, Sara, I can't forget how you felt in my arms. I can't forget the kisses."

She brushed at her ashen cheek. "Don't." Too often she had awakened from a dream of his kisses with an anguished cry of yearning.

"I've dated a lot of women, even thought about marrying a couple of them, but I couldn't block out the memory of you. I wanted to, but I couldn't. I had to find you to learn why."

"You...you had to find me? You didn't come here by chance?"

"No. I saw your books in a catalog and I saw your picture. I was astonished, to say the least, but also delighted at what you had accomplished. I bought your books and read them and enjoyed them. But it wasn't enough. It made the yearning to see you even stronger. So I called your publisher and got your address."

Her blue eyes widened with wonder. "But why?"

"I told you why! I must learn why I can't forget you! It's probably because I felt so guilty and needed to ask you, no, beg you, to forgive me. I needed to know that I hadn't ruined your life totally." He spread his hands, palms up. "And here you are, not ruined and ready to marry Roger Cairns."

She lifted her chin a fraction. "Are you surprised that I survived without you?"

"No." But was he? Disappointed, even? "But I'm thankful that I came at this time in your life so that I could help you through this difficulty."

"I appreciate your help. After this is all taken care of, you can go about your business without a thought of...me."

"Somehow I doubt that. You're impossible to forget."

A thrill passed through her and she ducked her head to hide the pleasure she felt.

"I'm thirty-one years old, Sara, and I want a wife and family. Something has always stopped me. *You* have always stopped me. At least the memory of you." He touched her hand and she jumped. "Please forgive me for hurting you all those years ago."

Suddenly she knew she could, with God's help. "I do, Boyd. I really do forgive you."

He leaped up and pulled her to her feet. "Thank you! You don't know what that means to me!"

His hands felt warm around hers and his gray eyes had a light she hadn't noticed before. She felt a strange emptiness now that her anger and bitterness toward him were gone. She smiled at his happiness and also because she suddenly felt light and free. She had not realized what a weight anger and bitterness and unforgiveness had been.

The telephone rang, shattering the moment. Reality struck and Sara ran to answer it. It was Amber.

"I got your message, Sara. What's up?"

"George called and said the police questioned him and he wants the money tomorrow so he can leave. He said if I don't give it to him, he'll hand Carlie over to Pete. And Pete is in the kiddy porn ring."

Amber's brain whirled with ideas. "I'll track George down today and have a heart-to-heart with him. In fact, I just might give him a big surprise."

"Be careful so he doesn't get angry and give Carlie to Pete as revenge," said Sara hoarsely.

"I'll call you after I talk to George."

Sara hung up and turned tearfully to Boyd. "Right now my faith seems terribly low."

He pulled her close and said against her fragrant hair, "God is your Father. He loves you and wants the best for you. He said if we believe we receive when we pray, that we'll have what we pray for. So, let's pray for Carlie right now."

She slipped her arms around Boyd and bowed her head with his.

* * *

At the Holiday Inn Amber phoned Deputy Sheriff Donally. "Anything new about Olga Swensen, Grace?"

"My men found her not more than an hour ago. Dead. Her car ran off the road and hit a tree just outside of town."

Amber shook her head. "An accident?"

"No way! It was made to look like one, but it was murder. Someone didn't want us talking to Olga."

"Did you speak to her at all?"

Grace sighed heavily. "No."

"What about George Palmer? I hear you questioned him."

"He seems clean, but we'll keep an eye on him."

"I want to talk to him. Where could I find him?"

Grace was quiet a long time. "Amber, I want you to stay out of this."

Amber rolled her eyes. "Sorry, Grace. I can't. It's imperative that I speak to him now. If you don't tell me where he is, I'll have to find out on my own. That will waste valuable time. But I'll do it if that's the way you want it."

With a sigh Grace said, "He's staying at Chambers Motel. Room 7. If you learn anything important, please let me know."

"I learned that Pete Snyder, out of prison a couple of months, is into kiddy porn and working with the ring here in town."

"Where's Snyder now?"

"I don't know. You might call his probation officer. I need to know when you find Pete Snyder and where. I must talk to him too."

"You work with me and I'll work with you."

"Thanks, Grace. I'm grateful for your help." Amber hung up with a satisfied smile. In all her years as a PI she'd never had police co-operation before from anyone but Sheriff Fritz Javor. But he

was special. She flipped back her mass of red hair
and ran to her car.

She found George without any trouble. At first
he growled at her to get away from his door, but
she pushed her way in and stood with her back to
the closed door. The room was a mess and smelled
closed in.

"Just who are you anyway?" George asked
angrily as he clicked off his blaring TV.

"I told you. Amber Ainslie. Sara hired me to stop
you. And you should be glad she did."

He slammed his fist into his palm. "She'll get it
for this!"

"No. She won't. But if you're not careful you
might end up dead just like Olga Swensen did."

He frowned, but he sank to the edge of the
unmade bed.

Amber perched on the edge of the dirty brown
chair and quickly told George about Olga's murder.
"So, George, you're playing hard ball. These
people will kill you as easily as they killed Olga if
you get in their way."

"But I'm getting out of town tomorrow."

"Even if Sara can't pay you?"

He growled deep in his throat.

"There are a lot of hours between now and
tomorrow morning."

"Why are you trying to scare me?"

"Because I want Carlie. I don't want her put in a
porn video. Do you? I don't want her to end up like
the boy I took to the hospital." Amber went into
great detail about the boy and she saw the horror in

George's eyes. "Is that what you want for Carlie?"

His shoulders sagged. "What do you want me to do?"

"Tell me where Carlie is so I can make sure she's safe. And tell me all you know about kiddy porn here in town."

"What's in it for me?"

"Your life." She drew a word picture of what could happen to him if he continued with his plan to turn Carlie over to the kiddy porn ring. "They won't let you out once you're involved. You know that. Pete Snyder knows that."

George nodded. "You're right."

"So, where's Carlie?" Inside Amber's nerves were jumping, but outwardly she looked calm and in control.

He jumped up and paced the small room, then told her the address where she would find Carlie. "The woman she lives with is a real witch. Watch out for her. If she knows you want Carlie she'll hide her so you never find her."

"Does she have a legal right to keep Carlie?"

"No. Ma just handed her over and old Hester Grove owed Ma a favor, so she took her. Hester said she'd find a way to make back the money Carlie would cost her."

"Is she into kiddy porn?"

"Not that I know of. But she might be."

"So you don't know if Carlie is all right?" Amber held her breath for the answer. Somehow Carlie had become very important to her.

"I saw Carlie a couple of months ago. She was

doing all right. As good as any kid that lives with Hester could."

"I'll get Carlie."

"What about me?" George thumped his chest.

"You leave today. I'll give you a name and address. It's a man in Ohio who will give you a job and a place to stay as long as you stay out of trouble with the law. Are you interested?"

He rubbed his jaw. His whiskers sounded raspy. Finally he nodded. He never had a chance before and he wasn't getting any younger. Maybe it was time he went straight. Sara had made it. Maybe he could too.

Amber jotted down the name and address and handed it over. "I'll be calling to make sure you get there. If you decide to stay here you'll be in danger not only from the porn gang, but also from me. I can get Sara to charge you with blackmail and you'll be in jail faster than you can blink." She stepped close to George and looked him square in the eye. "Got that?"

He nodded in defeat. "I'll leave now."

"Here's fifty for gas and food." She pushed the money into his hand and walked out to her car. She felt like leaping high and clicking her heels.

Chapter 6

Carlie yawned and stretched, then eased out from behind the couch. She was tired of staying in the teachers' lounge. It smelled like cigarette smoke and coffee. Maybe it was safe now to mix with the other kids. No one would notice.

She spotted half a doughnut on a napkin beside a cup of steaming coffee. Her stomach growled and she grabbed the doughnut and took a large bite. It tasted sweet and good.

Just then the door opened and Mrs. Tooker, the special reading teacher, walked in. She stopped short when she saw Carlie. "What are you doing here?"

Carlie tried to answer but she couldn't. Her mouth was full of the suddenly dry doughnut. Helplessly she shook her head and tried to step around Mrs. Tooker.

"Oh, no you don't! You're going right to the principal's office. I get tired of you children thinking you can invade the treachers' privacy." Mrs. Tooker caught Carlie's arm and marched her out into the hall.

Her heart thudding painfully against her ribs,

Carlie tried to break free, but Mrs. Tooker tightened her grip.

"Don't you make a scene, girl, or I'll call your parents to come get you," snapped Mrs. Tooker.

Carlie's heart sank and she walked quietly to the office. Was this the end for her?

* * *

Boyd stopped the car at the address Amber had given them. "This is it, Sara."

Her face was almost as white as the clouds in the sky. Butterflies fluttered wildly in her stomach. "How can I face her after ten years?"

"She's your daughter. She probably has waited all these years just for you to find her."

"Do you really think so?" Sara moistened her dry lips with the tip of her tongue. "I've dreamed of finding her and taking her home with me, but I never thought it could happen."

Boyd squeezed her icy hand. "We must be very careful with Hester Grove. We must handle this just like Amber told us."

"I can do it. I must!"

"I know you can." He squeezed her hand one last time, smiled and slipped out of the car. He walked with her to the door and knocked, waited and knocked again.

"No one's home," she whispered hoarsely. Her stomach felt full of heavy bricks.

"Let's look around," said Boyd. He led her around the small, run-down house to the backyard full of weeds and scraggly grass. There were ragged, uneven bushes along the house. The neighboring houses and yards looked the same.

"What kind of life did Carlie have here?" whispered Sara in anguish.

"I hate to think," he said.

"So do I." Sara's eyes filled with tears, but she blinked them away. Right now she couldn't cry. She had to find Carlie.

Boyd glanced at his watch. "Amber said to try Packard Elementary School if we couldn't find Hester Grove. Carlie's enrolled there under the name Carlie Grove."

Sara groaned. "She probably doesn't even know her last name is Palmer." Sara hadn't listed Pete as the father because he said she'd be sorry if she did. By the way he treated others, she knew that she'd better not cross him. He had been nice to her until she wouldn't have an abortion. Oh, how foolish she was to become involved with him!

"We'll find a telephone and call the school like Amber said to do." said Boyd.

Sara bit her lip and nodded. "I don't know if I can say what I must say."

Boyd slipped an arm lightly around her shoulders and led her to the car. "You can do whatever it takes, Sara."

"Yes. Yes, I can," she whispered around the lump in her throat.

At the pay phone near the Shell Station Boyd called the Packard Elementary School and Sara took the receiver from him, her hand stiff and icy. She cleared her throat. When a woman answered Sara said in a hurried voice, "This is Hester Grove. I'm sending Boyd Collier and Sara Palmer to pick Carlie up now. You take her out of class and have her ready in the office. This is a family emergency." Sara hung up before the woman could ask any questions, then weakly walked to the car with Boyd. In silence he drove to the school and parked.

"Oh, Boyd, I think I'm going to be sick." Sara leaned her head weakly against the dash.

He patted her shoulder. "No, you're not. God is with you. You have His strength, not your own."

She lifted her head and dabbed perspiration off her forehead and upper lip. "Yes. Yes, God is my strength!"

"Shall we go inside?" asked Boyd softly.

She nodded.

Slowly they walked through the wide doors and into the office. Sara's heels clicked against the tile floor. Her skirt swayed around her legs. She pushed a tissue into her suit jacket pocket, squared her shoulders and glanced at Boyd. He looked very handsome and business-like in his gray suit and white shirt. He touched the knot of his paisley tie.

"We're here to pick up Carlie Grove," said Boyd. "I'm Boyd Collier and this is Sara Palmer. Hester Grove spoke to you on the phone." Amber had told him to give as little information as possible. If they questioned him about picking up Carlie, he'd give them more information. But they didn't question him. Maybe they were used to strangers picking up Carlie. The secretary turned to a woman standing near a file cabinet.

"Get Carlie, will you, Patty? She's in the office."

Patty nodded and walked away.

Sara wanted to hold Boyd's hand but she stood beside him with a slight smile pasted in place. She caught the smell of newly copied papers in a pile on the counter.

"Carlie was in the teachers' lounge where she didn't belong. She was sent to the principal's office as punishment," explained the secretary.

Patty walked out of the office with a hand around Carlie's arm. Sara trembled, staring at the ragged, thin girl with Patty. Boyd steadied her with a hand at her waist.

Her head down, Carlie walked with Patty. She had been caught about fifteen minutes ago and she had no strength left to fight. She looked up expecting to see Ma, but instead she saw a man and woman she didn't know. She stiffened and tried to pull away from Patty. Had Perkins sent them to get her?

"Hello, Carlie," said Boyd gently.

"Carlie," whispered Sara with tears in her eyes.

Carlie stared at them without speaking. She didn't know them but, for some reason, she wasn't afraid of them. Patty pushed her to Boyd and he took her hand and walked out of the office with her. Sara followed, barely able to walk. After all these years, she finally had her baby.

Or was this another dream?

It seemed real. The breeze that blew against her as she walked to Boyd's car felt real. The smell of wood smoke in the air smelled real. The chatter of a bluejay sounded real.

Boyd opened the car door and Carlie slid across the front seat to sit in the middle.

"Where are you taking me?" asked Carlie in a small voice. Maybe she should have run away once they stepped outside the school. For some reason she hadn't wanted to run.

"Sara?" asked Boyd.

Sara swallowed hard. "We...we are taking you...home."

Carlie shivered. "To Ma's? Don't take me there!"

Sara silently begged Boyd for help.

He barely nodded, then patted Carlie's arm. "Don't be frightened. I know this is going to be a surprise to you, but this woman is Sara Palmer. She's your real mother."

Carlie gasped and Sara burst into tears.

"We'll go somewhere where we can talk privately," said Boyd. He drove away from the school, feeling some of the same weakness Sara felt.

Carlie looked up at him, her eyes wide in her small face. "Are you my real dad?"

"No. I'm Sara's friend."

"Oh. How come she's crying?"

"She's thought about you all these years and she wanted you, but never knew where you were until today."

"Oh." Carlie watched Sara as she tried to stop her tears. They did have the same color hair. When Sara dried her eyes and wiped her nose Carlie asked, "Are you really my mom?"

"Yes. Your name is Carlie Noreen Palmer. My

name is Sara Noreen Palmer."

"How come you made me live with that bad Hester Grove?"

"I didn't have a choice."

"It's a long story," said Boyd. "But we'll tell you all about it."

"She didn't want me," said Carlie. "So I ran away from Ma and Perkins. I hid."

Sara and Boyd exchanged looks over Carlie's head.

"Who is Perkins?" asked Boyd as he pulled onto the expressway to head back to Chambers.

"I don't know. A man Ma talked to." Carlie turned to Sara. "Do I still have to call her Ma like she said?"

"No. No, you don't"

"What do you want me to call you?"

"Mom would be fine."

Carlie nodded. "Mom." She turned to Boyd. "What do I call you?"

"Boyd would be fine," he said with a grin. "My name is Boyd Collier."

Sara suddenly realized how bad Carlie smelled and how unkempt she looked. "Boyd, let's stop at a mall and buy some clothes for Carlie, shall we?"

Boyd nodded. He had been thinking the same thing. He knew there was a nice mall at the next exit. He pulled off and parked in the large parking lot. "Carlie and I will wait here while you go inside."

Sara checked the tag at the collar of Carlie's shirt and the one on her jeans for sizes. "Be back right away. Later we'll shop together, Carlie."

"But I can't go in stinking like I do," said Carlie.
"I never had a bath for days and days."

"You can take one at my house," said Sara. She
opened the car door and a pleasant breeze blew in.
"I'll buy jeans and a sweater for now. Any special
color of sweater, Carlie?"

"Red." Carlie sighed. "I never had a new red
sweater before."

"Red it is." Sara ran across the lot and into the
mall. She found the children's department in the
first store she came to and bought underwear, socks,
a sweater and jeans. Quickly she paid for them and
ran back to the car. Through the years she'd looked
through the children's department longing to buy
clothes for Carlie. Once when Carlie was about five
she'd bought a little girl's dress and hid it away in
her dresser. It was still there.

* * *

Amber sank low in the seat of her car as a man
walked to the door of the house she'd had under
surveillance since she sent Boyd and Sara after Carlie. She knew where the men were living, but didn't
question them for fear of scaring them away. She
wanted to know who their contact was. The man at
the door fit Perkins Weeze's description. Now she
could call Grace Donally to pick up Weeze as well
as the men. With Jaz Knobb's testimony against
Weeze, he would be convicted. And Weeze might
tell about the head of the ring here in Chambers.
She would find the kids that Midge Sawyer had

hired her to find. Amber hoped to have this case wrapped up so she could be home by tomorrow night. Perhaps Mina would have good news about finding a country home, one with plenty of rooms and a wonderful yard.

She smiled as she picked up her car phone to call Grace Donally.

* * *

Roger took a deep breath and stepped into Neddie's apartment building. He had promised himself to stay calm no matter what she said about her feelings for Boyd Collier. For the past two hours Roger had tried to call Sara to see if she would talk him out of going to Neddie's. Sara hadn't answered her phone.

Neddie opened the apartment door and tugged Roger inside. "You sounded so desperate on the phone," she said breathlessly. "Have you found out what's been upsetting Sara?"

Roger frowned. "Has something been?"

"Yes! Didn't you notice how tense she's been?"

"Well, I suppose I have."

"Boyd said..." Neddie's voice trailed away as she walked across the living room and sank to the couch. Boyd had said that Sara didn't really love Roger, but she couldn't tell Roger that. It would hurt him too much.

Roger rattled the change in his pocket. "Just what did Boyd say?"

"Oh, a lot of things. He's known Sara a long time."

"Sometimes I wonder about her past but she won't talk about it. Has she said anything to you?"

"No. It must have been pretty sad, though."

Roger sat beside Neddie. He suddenly realized how easy it was to relax at her place. Maybe it was the pleasant muted colors she decorated with. He liked the bouquet of flowers on the coffee table. He sighed heavily. "I tried to call Sara, but she was gone. I wonder if she's with Boyd Collier."

Neddie plucked at the sleeve of her yellow blouse. Boyd had said that he was going to have a serious talk with Sara. Maybe he took her away from her house and her phone so they wouldn't be disturbed.

"You like him, don't you?" said Roger almost accusingly.

Neddie nodded. "Don't you?"

"I don't know. Oh, I suppose I do. It's just that he kind of takes over no matter where he is." Roger rubbed an unsteady hand across his cheek. He felt the rasp of whiskers. "Like he did with you at Rita Hardy's party."

Neddie shrugged. "He was being kind. He knew I felt out of place."

"Out of place? You?"

"I'm a bank teller, Roger. The other people there were business associates of Sara and Rita's."

"And friends from church."

"Most of them business people."

"I wish you wouldn't get so down on yourself. You're a wonderful person."

Her heart skipped a beat and she jumped up. She

dare not let him see how she felt about him no matter what Boyd had said. It wasn't right. "Would you like a cup of coffee?"

* * *

Sara walked out of the grocery store and stopped short. Pete stood just outside the door. He wore faded jeans that sagged on his lean hips and a navy blue sweatshirt that hung on his thin body. His long, light brown hair needed to be washed. He rubbed his hands over the side of his face and the tattoos on his arms. He looked much older than he was. Sara shivered and almost dropped the bag of groceries. She wanted to look toward Boyd's car where he and Carlie waited for her but knew if she looked, Pete would too. She dare not let him see Carlie!

"You're lookin' good, Sara," said Pete, grinning.

"George said you were out."

Pete's face hardened. "Never to go back!"

"So you're going straight."

"Who said?" He laughed and flipped his straggly hair back. "I been trying to find George."

"I don't know where he is."

"He said to meet him here an hour ago. But who do I see instead?" Pete chuckled and Sara shivered. "I almost didn't recognize you. George said you looked different—clean and pretty."

"I am different," said Sara stiffly. "I'm not the same girl who hung around you."

"You're all grown up, that's for sure." His eyes narrowed. "What about Carlie?"

Sara's blood turned to ice. "What about her?"

"You see her since your ma took her away from you?"

"Have you?"

"Once before I got sent away. She's a real cutie."

Sara gripped the bag of groceries tighter. "Pete, you wouldn't let anyone use her in porn pictures, would you?"

"Me?" He patted his thin chest. "How can you ask me such a question?"

"George said you were into kiddy porn."

Pete scowled. "And you ran right to the cops with that bit of info, didn't you?"

"I should have! But I didn't." She wanted to look toward the car to make sure Boyd and Carlie weren't coming to see about her. "But I will if you try to see Carlie!"

"She's as much mine as yours."

"You didn't want her! Your name's not even on her birth certificate."

"So?"

"So, she is not as much yours as mine."

"I know where she's at."

"What?"

"Hester Grove has her. I know old Hester. She's a long way from a saint and she wouldn't think twice about handing Carlie over to me. As long as old Hester got a few dollars for it."

Sara wanted to walk away, but she couldn't lead Pete to Boyd and Carlie. Abruptly she turned and walked back toward the door of the store. Before she reached it Pete caught her arm and spun her around. His face was dark with anger and she shivered. She wanted to call out or run, but she couldn't do anything that would bring Boyd or Carlie.

"Don't try to walk away from me as if I'm a nobody. A nothing!"

"I have to go," she said stiffly.

"You're going the wrong way."

"I forgot to get orange juice."

"And you happen to remember it right in the middle of our talk. Give me a break, Sara."

"I have things to do, Pete."

He leaned down close until she could smell his onion breath. "You're afraid somebody's going to see you talking to me, ain't you?"

"Leave me alone!"

"George told me you didn't want anyone knowing about your life here."

"It doesn't matter any more."

"What do you mean by that?"

She wanted to bite out her tongue. She managed to shrug nonchalantly. "My true friends won't care about my past."

"Ha!" Pete rolled his eyes. "Did you get dumb all of a sudden? It's only folks like us that don't care. But folks who live in nice houses and drive nice cars and have nice clothes, they look at things different. They don't like low class."

"I have to go, Pete."

"I'll drop by and see you sometime."

"No!"

"We'll have us a long talk about old times. And about Carlie." He looked at his watch and frowned.

"It's been fun, but I gotta run, Sara."

She pressed her mouth tightly shut to keep back a scream as he walked to a new yellow car and drove away. She waited until he turned the corner, then ran to Boyd's car, dropped the bag of groceries on the back seat and slipped in beside Carlie.

"What's wrong?" Boyd asked in alarm.

"Nothing."

Carlie twisted her finger around her shirt. She saw the fear on Sara's face and felt it all around her. "Did somebody hurt you?"

"I'm all right. Let's get out of here, Boyd."

He drove to her house in silence. With Carlie beside him, he couldn't question Sara further.

Later, as Sara put away the groceries, she told Boyd about Pete. Carlie was soaking in the bathtub.

"It's not safe for the two of you to stay here," he said. He pushed his hands into his pockets to keep from flinging her over his shoulder and taking her and Carlie to safety. "I'll take you home with me."

She nodded. "We probably should leave here." She turned away from him, her heart racing. "But I don't know about staying with you."

"Where else would you go? At my place I can keep you both safe. It's a big house with plenty of room for all three of us. It's the only answer, Sara."

She sighed and finally said, "All right."

"I'm going to call Amber. I want her to know what happened." Boyd called the Holiday Inn and left an urgent message for Amber to call Sara the minute she could. He left his number. He turned back to Sara and managed to smile. "There. Amber will take care of everything."

Sara walked to the bathroom to check on Carlie. The door was open and Carlie was standing in front of the mirror looking at herself dressed in clean, new clothes. Her hair was clean, brushed and shiny. "You look beautiful," said Sara softly.

"I do, don't I?" said Carlie, still looking in the mirror. She gingerly touched her red sweater and fingered the ends of her hair. "I thought I was ugly."

"You're not." Tears sparkling in her eyes, Sara squatted down so that they were the same height. They studied each other in the mirror. "See how much alike we look," whispered Sara. "Same blue eyes. Same dark hair."

Carlie slowly turned to Sara. "Are you really my mom? Really? No lie?"

Sara nodded. "I am. I was fifteen when you were born. When you were four months old my mom took you away from me and kicked me out of the house. I wanted you so badly, but she wouldn't let me have you and she wouldn't let me go back home. So I lived with Boyd's family. He was in college and they were lonely and wanted me. They loved me." She touched Carlie's soft cheek. "They would have loved you too, but Ma wouldn't tell them where you were and they couldn't get you. Besides, they thought you were with someone who loved you. And so did I."

"Ma didn't love me," whispered Carlie.

"I am so sorry!"

"Will you love me?"

"I never stopped loving you," Sara told her. "I dreamed about you many times and I prayed for you."

"What about my dad?"

Sara stood slowly. She sat on the edge of the tub and took Carlie's hands in hers. "His name is Pete Snyder and he's been in prison for dealing in drugs. He's not a nice person." She smoothed down Carlie's hair. "I'm sorry."

"Me too. I always had daydreams about my real mom and dad and in my daydreams they were both perfect."

Sara dabbed away a tear. "I wish it was true."

Carlie shrugged. "Ma was gonna sell me to Perkins."

"What?" cried Sara.

"So I ran away and hid. But I'm glad I got caught so you could find me instead of Ma or Perkins."

Sara turned to call to Boyd but he stood just outside the bathroom door. He had come when he heard her outburst. "She was going to sell Carlie to Perkins!"

"I heard."

"But I ran," said Carlie trying to reassure Sara. "I wouldn't let him buy me. I ran and you found me."

Sara pulled Carlie close and held her as if she'd never, ever let her go.

Chapter 7

Amber twirled her empty soda glass as she listened to Grace Donally who sat across the small table from her. The diner was almost empty this late in the evening. She knew they closed at nine.

Grace took a deep breath. "I know you don't want to hear this, but none of them would talk. None of them would admit to knowing where the kids are, nor admit to any connection with kiddy porn. Perkins Weese says Jaz Knobb has a grudge against him and lied."

Amber felt her temper rise in frustration, but she kept it in control. "So?"

"So they got a good lawyer and I had to let them go."

"I can't believe this!"

"I know. Sometimes the system stinks." Grace pushed her coffee mug away from her and rested her elbows on the small table. "It would make my day if I could just figure out who is head of this kiddy porn ring. It's not Weese. He's not smart enough."

"What about George Palmer?" asked Amber. It had been a little too easy to talk him into going out of town. As soon as she finished talking with Grace, she would call down to Ohio and see if good old George had checked in.

"He's small-time." Grace waved her hand as if she was brushing away a fly. "Maybe your client knows."

"I doubt it." Amber couldn't imagine Midge Sawyer keeping that a secret. But then, who knows? Maybe she could.

"Your client might be afraid to tell you. Or be too loyal."

"Loyal?"

"Maybe he cares about the top guy."

Amber hid a smile. Midge cared about her husband. Amber hooked her hair behind her ear. She couldn't imagine Pastor Ted Sawyer as head of kiddy porn—not because he was a pastor, but because he had a genuine love for God and for people. Maybe Midge was protecting someone else. Was it possible? But who? "It is food for thought," she said with a slight nod.

"Who is your client, Amber? I must know!"

Amber sighed heavily. "I'm sorry." She pushed back from the table, then grinned. "I'll get going before we have a fight. I'm not going to tell you and you know it."

Sighing, Grace stood and picked up her purse. "Talk to you tomorrow."

"Did you put anyone on Weeze or the other guys?"

Grace nodded. "But they probably know it. And they'll be careful who they see."

"Or they'll give your people the slip."

"That's been known to happen." Grace lifted her hand in a wave and walked outdoors to her car.

Amber walked to the pay phone in the corner away from the only two people in the place. A rock song blared from a radio in the kitchen.

She held the receiver tightly to her ear as she listened to it ring. On the fifth ring a man answered. "Johnny? Amber Ainslie here."

"How's it going, Amber?"

"Don't ask. Did my guy show up there?"

"Nope. A couple of others did, but not George Palmer."

Amber sagged against the wall. "Oh, Johnny," she whispered.

"You don't think he's just late, do you?"

"No. And I thought he was serious about leaving here. But if he does show up, give me a call." She told him the number of her motel and said goodbye. She would have to tell Sara Palmer the bad news. Maybe Sara already knew.

Amber dropped in change and dialed Sara's number. The phone rang ten times before she hung up. Coins rattled down into the coin return. She fished them out and used them again, this time to call the Holiday Inn for her messages. She was to return calls to Mina Streebe, Fritz Javor, Midge Sawyer and Sara Palmer at Boyd Collier's number.

"Wonder why she's at Boyd's?" muttered Amber as she slowly walked to her car. Did it have something to do with George?

She called Midge with her car phone as she drove toward the motel. She wanted to call Fritz and

Mina in the comfort of her room.

Midge answered breathlessly on the first ring.

"Amber here, Midge."

"I can't talk here. I'll meet you at your motel in a few minutes." She sounded frantic.

"Fine." Amber frowned as she hung up, then called Sara. Boyd answered on the second ring. "Boyd? Amber."

"Thank God you finally called! We have Carlie," he said. "She's asleep upstairs. Sara's going to the kitchen phone so we can both talk to you."

By the time they finished telling all their news she pulled into her parking place at the motel. "So, Carlie said Perkins was going to *buy* her from Hester Grove."

"Yes," said Sara with a shudder.

Amber drummed her fingers on the steering wheel. "But she didn't know why?"

"No," said Boyd.

"I'm so thankful we got her before he did," said Sara.

"Me too," said Amber. "I'm glad you and Carlie are staying at Boyd's. Boyd, call Grace Donally and tell her what you told me. Ask if she can have a squad car drive regularly past your place. Tell her what Pete said about meeting George."

"I thought you said George was leaving town," said Sara as a shiver of fear trickled down her back.

"He didn't get to Ohio, so keep your eyes open for him."

"Pete must've gotten to him," said Sara wildly. "Pete could always talk George into anything."

"Tell Grace that," said Amber as she watched Midge Sawyer pull up beside her. "And Sara, you charge George with blackmail so Grace can arrest him when she does find him."

"Yes. Yes, I will!" Sara knew keeping Carlie safe was more important than having people learn of her past. Suddenly it didn't matter if anyone knew about her. She and her baby were safe.

"Call me if you need anything." Amber waved at Midge to let her know she saw her park. Midge looked ready to fly into a million pieces. "Sara, I'm glad you found Carlie."

"Me too," whispered Sara.

"Me too," said Boyd hoarsely.

Amber hung up and hurried to Midge's car. "What's up?" she asked as Midge opened her door.

Midge burst into tears and sagged against the open car door. "I can't keep this up."

Amber forced back her impatience and patted Midge on the shoulder. "Tell me what happened."

"Mrs. Drift."

Amber froze. "What about her?"

"She called this afternoon."

"And?"

"She asked for Ted and I said he'd be gone until late tonight." Midge rubbed her eyes. "He just got home. He was in the shower when you called, so I slipped away. I didn't want him to know about you working for me."

Amber closed her eyes and tried to count to ten to hold her temper. She only made it to five. "What did Mrs. Drift want? Did you ask her where she was calling from? Is there a number where I can reach her?"

Midge nervously pushed back her short curls and looked ready to jump out of her skin. "I've never had to deal with anything like this before. Ted takes care of the problems and I take care of Ted. Oh, why did I overhear Mrs. Drift in the first place? I hate knowing things! And I couldn't make her stop talking. She told me what she wanted to tell Ted. I did not want to hear any of it!"

Amber wanted to tell Midge to grow up, but she actually understood her actions. Aunt Sharon was the same way. She let Uncle Brian handle every detail of their lives and if she accidently learned anything that was upsetting she'd fall apart. Amber knew how patient all of them had to be with Aunt Sharon and she knew she would need the same patience with Midge Sawyer. Taking a deep breath, Amber slipped her arm around Midge. "You just tell me what Mrs. Drift said and I'll take care of it. After you tell me you can go back home to your husband. Start at the beginning and tell me everything. Maybe you'll feel better if we sit down. We can go inside or sit in the car."

"I'll tell you quickly so I can leave." Midge shuddered. "I wish I would have told Ted what I overheard in the first place. He could have done something."

"But you didn't tell Ted. You called me instead."

"I know." Midge picked at the pink fingernail polish on her thumb. "I made such a mistake!"

"But you did something anyway. You should be

proud of yourself for wanting to help even if you were frightened. It took a lot of courage to call me for help in finding those kids that Mrs. Drift talked about." Silently Amber thanked God for the help He was giving her in dealing with Midge. Only God's grace kept her from screaming at Midge.

Midge fumbled in her purse for a tissue, wiped her eyes and blew her nose. A pickup drove past with a load of laughing teens in the back. A cool breeze sent a paper skittering across the parking lot to land against the back tire of a white Cadillac. In the distance a siren wailed.

Amber waited, her hands deep in her sweater pockets.

Midge trembled, squared her shoulders and faced Amber. "Mrs. Drift didn't leave town after all."

"What?" Amber miraculously kept her voice down.

"She left today."

"So what she told you is new information?"

"Yes."

"Did you know she was still in town?"

Midge shook her head.

"What did she tell you?"

"Mrs. Drift said that she heard the men talk about a place where they shot the videos of the kids. She was afraid to tell until she heard that Olga Swensen had been killed. She wanted to make sure the kids were found and the men caught before more people died. She felt safe in calling now because she was flying to another country where nobody could track her down and try to kill her."

"Where is the house?"

"I wrote it down." Midge pulled a slip of paper from the front pocket of her slacks. "Here."

Amber read the address, then pushed it into the pocket of her sweater. "Did she identify any of the people involved?"

"The two men that the police arrested."

"No one else?"

"No."

"What else did she say?"

Midge bit her lower lip. "She said they were going to do only a couple more videos before they moved on. They had orders to get out after the Charity Fair because a private detective was getting too close."

Amber frowned. "Too close?" She didn't feel too close to anything. "Too close to what?"

"Too close to the truth."

"What Charity Fair?"

"For the Burn Center. Rita Hardy and Sara Palmer are working on it."

"Why would the Charity Fair have anything to do with kiddy porn?"

Midge shrugged. "I'm just telling you what Mrs. Drift said."

"How did Mrs. Drift happen to hear all of this?"

Midge bit her lower lip. "One of the men, Abe Keeler, is her cousin. She stayed with him after she got out of the hospital."

Amber sucked in air. She knew Keeler was the short, bald man that she'd seen. "Did you know they were cousins?"

"No."

"So she heard all of this and her cousin, Abe Keeler, was just going to let her walk away scot-free?"

"She said she pretended to be too weak to walk, so they didn't think she was going anywhere. When her cousin left, she drove to the airport and flew to Chicago. She used a different name so they couldn't track her down. She said from Chicago she was flying to a different country. She called me from Chicago."

"Is it true? Or is she just saying it and staying here?"

"I heard noises in the background that sounded like the airport. But it could have been any airport, I suppose." Midge twisted her fingers together. "Oh, I don't know! But she desperately wanted to see those kids get away from the men. She said she could not handle knowing what was happening."

"Anything else?"

"She sounded very frightened." Midge patted her racing heart. "I must go before Ted worries about me."

"Midge, tell Ted all of this."

"I can't!"

"Why?"

"He'd be very upset that I eavesdropped in the first place."

"He would be proud of you for helping stop kiddy porn. And it was you who saved the little boy that I found. Without your help I wouldn't have found him and he would be dead."

Midge nodded slightly.

"So tell your husband, then you don't have it hanging over you. Honesty is important in a relationship. You know that." Amber knew she sounded as if she was speaking to a child.

Midge trembled. "You're right, of course."

"You had the courage to come to me for help; you'll have the courage to talk to Ted." Amber smiled and patted Midge's arm. "You can do it!"

"I don't know."

"You can, Midge!"

"Do you really think so?"

"I know so."

Midge squared her shoulders. "I will!"

"Good for you. He might want you to tell all of this to the police."

"And should I?"

"Yes. To Grace Donally. You know her."

Midge nodded. "I can talk to her without being too frightened. Thank you, Amber! You've been a bigger help to me than you realize."

"Thank you."

"But I don't want you to quit working on this case just because I talk to Grace. You find those kids, Amber. You see that they get away from those terrible people!"

"I will." Amber studied Midge thoughtfully. "Do you have any idea who is the head of the porn ring here in town?"

"No. If I knew I'd tell you!"

Amber believed her.

A few minutes later Midge drove away and Amber went inside her room to call Mina Streebe.

"It's about time you called, Amber," Mina said in her sharp manner. "I have news that can't wait."

Amber chuckled as she sat cross-legged in the middle of her bed. "You always do, Mina. What is it this time?"

"Bob Hardy."

Amber gripped the phone tightly. "What about him?"

"Pete Snyder worked for him five years ago in between prison sentences."

"You don't say!"

"He did the yard work around the commercial real estate that Bob Hardy had listed."

"Good work, Mina."

"That's not all." Mina fluffed her dyed red frizzy curls. She pulled her flowered blouse over the plaid pants she had found in the back of her closet.

"What else, Mina?" Amber eased out of her warm sweater. Mina loved to make her drag information out of her.

"I found Sara Palmer's mother. She told me Carlie is with a woman named Hester Grove. She said Hester called to tell her Carlie had run away, but she didn't plan to call the police because of all the trouble it could cause."

"We have Carlie. Sara Palmer found her at school just this afternoon."

"Good. And did you know Pete Snyder, the same Pete Snyder who worked for Bob Hardy, is Carlie's father?"

"I know it. And he's into kiddy porn."

"You don't say!" Mina whistled. "Sara's mother didn't say anything about that. But she did say that Pete is one bad dude."

"What about George Palmer?"

"His mother said he and Pete have been thick for years. She hasn't heard from him since last week."

"How did you get her to talk so freely?"

Mina chuckled. "Not so free, Amber. We paid her back electric bill. She said she would help for nothing, but times were hard for her and she needed help."

"Does her information check out?"

"Yep."

"Anything on Bob Hardy?"

"Nothing I could find. But I thought I'd dig a little deeper just in case."

"Check on his wife too. Rita Hardy."

"I've already started."

"Good. Anything else?"

"Not on the case. But I found a house that I'm going to look at tomorrow. Sounds good and there's room for both of us."

Amber sighed and shook her head. Mina was determined to stick to her like velcro. She wanted a place of her own and Mina knew it. "Mina, let's not go into that again."

"You're too busy *not* to have me there to keep your house clean and your meals fixed."

"We've already settled this, Mina."

"Talk to you tomorrow." Mina laughed and hung up.

Amber called Fritz Javor at home, but hung up

after twelve rings. She would try again about midnight. He was probably out with one of his many women friends. A pang of jealousy jabbed her but she forced it away as she pulled the address from her sweater pocket. She opened the city map that she had bought just after hitting town and looked up the address. "Only a few blocks from the other house," she muttered. Was this a set-up? She would be very careful that she didn't walk into a trap.

Several minutes later she drove slowly past the house. It was in the slum district and the house was in bad shape like the other houses around it. Lights shone from under shades on the front windows. A car was parked in the short drive. Weeds instead of grass grew in the cluttered yard. A few trees and bushes were scattered up and down the street and in some of the yards. Two young trees stood in the yard of the house she was investigating. She checked to see the best approach to the house, then decided to sneak around back and peek in the windows. No one walked the streets and only an occasional car drove past. As far as she could tell, the police did not have the house staked out. Either their undercover work was good or the men had given them the slip.

She parked half a block away and walked back toward the house with her sweater buttoned and a dark cap pulled over her bright hair. She wore hightop black sneakers and black jeans that fit snugly against her long legs. Her senses were alert. Unconsciously her mind was working on the information gathered in the past few days. Somewhere there was a solution to the case.

If *they*—whoever *they* were—were nervous about her getting too close, then she'd better figure out what had made them think that. It wasn't enough merely to find the kids and get them to safety. She also wanted to nail the top jerk who would dare to make money off innocent children in such a horrible way.

She shivered as she slipped up close to the house. A twig cracked under her foot and she stopped, held her breath and waited. Muted sounds of music came from inside. In the distance a dog barked. She smelled the can of garbage that stood near the cracked sidewalk.

In the back of the house she peered in each window but saw nothing. She peeked under the shade in the windows with the lights, but couldn't make out anything. Finally Amber walked back to her car and opened the trunk. She pulled out a brown curly wig, a bright yellow and pink sweater that almost reached her knees, tinted glasses, an old red purse that was big enough to hold the state of Michigan and a pair of red high-heeled boots. In a few minutes not even Fritz Javor would have recognized her.

She walked boldly to the door and knocked loudly, then knocked again.

Chapter 8

Amber pounded hard on the door with her fist. Her heart pounded just as hard against her ribcage. "Keep me safe, Jesus," she whispered.

Abe Keeler jerked open the door and she pushed right in with a bold laugh. "Tell Tina I'm here, will you, mister?"

"Tina?"

Amber playfully punched Keeler's arm. "Hey, don't play games with me, guy. Tina said to meet her here before eleven, so tell her I'm here."

"You got the wrong house, lady," snapped Keeler. He tried to push her out, but she brushed him aside and walked further into the room. A couch sat against one wall with an overstuffed chair pulled up near a cheap coffee table. The room smelled of coffee, cigarettes and body odor.

Amber called, "Hey, Tina, come on out here! It's me. Betsy. Don't you joke me, Tina!" She listened for sounds of children and looked around to see if she could find any clues while all the time acting like she was totally without brains.

Keeler grabbed her arm and scowled. Perspiration glistened on his bald head. "You get out of here! You got the wrong house."

"Don't joke me," Amber said with a loud laugh.

"I mean it, lady! You got the wrong house."

Just then Pete Snyder stepped from another room into the front room, carefully closing the connecting door behind him. "What's going on?" he snapped.

Amber twisted away from Keeler and ran to Pete. "Hey, you're Tina's hunk, ain't you? She said she was going with a guy that would jerk your heart right out of your body. It's gotta be you. She has a thing for tattoos." Amber ran her finger over the snake that crawled along Pete's right arm.

Pete pushed her hand away. "Get her out of here, Abe."

Keeler stepped toward her, but she jumped behind the overstuffed chair and giggled.

"You tell Tina I'm here and I'll leave when she comes out." Amber pushed the tinted glasses up on her nose. "Not before. And I can be very stubborn. She always says that." Amber giggled again.

"Get her out of here," snapped Pete.

Amber lifted her chin. "Tina said to meet her here and I'm gonna do just that."

Pete turned to Keeler. "You know a Tina?"

"No. But maybe George does."

Amber's heart jerked and a shiver crawled down her spine. So George was here!

Pete turned to the door. "Get in here, George."

George Palmer walked in, his shirt unbuttoned and the belt on his jeans dangling. He stopped short when he saw Amber. "Who's this?"

"I'm supposed to meet Tina here," said Amber in her ditzy blond voice. She wanted to slap George silly for not going to Ohio where he could start a new life, but she didn't let any of that show.

"She come to help?" asked George.

"Tina didn't say nothin' about helpin'. We was going for pizza."

"Do you know a Tina, George?" asked Pete.

George frowned thoughtfully. "What about the girl we had in here last week?"

"Cindy was her name," said Keeler.

Amber flung her giant red bag over her shoulder. "I'm sure getting tired of this whole thing. You tell Tina to get out here or I'll go back and get her." She started for the door that led into the room that Pete and George had come from, but suddenly they all three blocked her way. She shook her finger at them. "Now, that's not fair. Three against one. I want to find Tina and you won't let me get her." She tried to push through them as she shouted, "Tina, they won't let me in!"

"You're leaving now," snapped Pete. "Abe, George, get her out of here."

They reached for her, but she jumped back. So, they had something in there that they didn't want her to see. Were they right in the middle of making a disgusting video? She held her hand out to them, to keep them at arm's length. "You tell Tina I'm mad at her. If she wants me, she'll just have to call. Betsy don't play games! You tell Tina that!" Amber flung her giant purse over her other shoulder and sashayed out the door and down the walk, her boot heels loud in the sudden silence behind her. At the curb she turned and called to the men standing in the doorway, "If you're joking, you'll be sorry."

They slammed the door and in the darkness she ran to her car. Trembling, she pulled off her disguise and quickly slipped on a wind-blown-looking black wig that barely reached her shoulders, round tinted glasses with light blue frames, a silky blue blouse with a leather vest and flat black leather slipons with blue flowered anklets. She rolled her jeans up two cuffs, slipped on five gaudy rings, grabbed a tiny black purse and walked back to the front door. She knocked a small, hesitant knock, waited, then knocked again.

Pete flung open the door.

"You're Pete, right?" Amber spoke in a New York accent. "Is Betsy here yet? I'm Tina."

Pete jabbed his fingers through his hair. "What's going on here? How do you know who I am?"

"He said I'd know you by your tattoos and long hair." Amber stepped into the room and looked around. Pete was the only one in sight. "I thought Betsy would be here by now. I told her you were my man so she wouldn't suspect anything."

"What're you talking about?" asked Pete helplessly.

"Betsy thinks we're going out for pizza, but we really came to work."

"Work?"

Amber frowned at Pete. "I talked to Jaz Knobb just last week in Bradsville. He said Perkins Weese would give me a job if I'd stop by. I told him I'd be out of state for a few days, but would work when I got back."

"Knobb's in jail."

"No! I can't believe it!" She looked around as if she was frightened. "I'd better get. Tell Betsy it's all off. It would be the end for me if I was arrested." She started for the door. Pete stopped her.

"Are you a model?"

"You crazy? I don't do that stuff. I'm a photographer."

Amber saw the baffled look on Pete's face before he turned and shouted, "Abe, George, get in here."

She watched as Abe and George came in, then stopped short and stared at her.

"Who is she?" asked George nervously.

"She says she came to work," said Pete, rubbing his hand down his faded sweatshirt. "She's a photographer."

She stepped forward without a smile. "I'm Tina. Betsy was to come work with me, but she's late. I can't start without her; she has my stuff in her car. But if you want to show me my *subjects,* I can start planning. Kids don't always do what you want when you want."

"I don't know what's going on here," said Abe Keeler. "Perkins never said a word to me."

Amber turned on him and said in an icy voice, "Should he? You the boss or something?"

Keeler shrugged and backed away.

"Something funny is going on here," said Pete with a scowl.

"You could always call Perkins Weese," Amber

snapped with a wave of her hand. Light flashed off her rings. "Call him. He never minds questions." She leaned toward Pete. "Does he?"

George laughed nervously. "Perkins has no patience for questions and we all know it."

"Show me where I'm to work and by then Betsy should be here." Amber stepped toward Pete. "Don't make me take all night for this, Pete. I want to sleep sometime, you know."

"You sure you can trust her, Pete?" asked Keeler.

Amber saw Pete's hesitation and she tapped his shoulder. "If it's too hard for you to make up your own mind, I'm going. I don't need this, you know."

Pete rattled his keys in his pockets and finally nodded. "I'll show you the kids and the room, but we aren't shooting again until Thursday."

She stopped short. "Why didn't you say so before this? I could've been out of here by now." She frowned down at her watch. "Where *is* Betsy? Sometimes I wonder why I put up with such an airhead."

"She came a while ago," said George.

Amber flung out her hand in disgust. "Why didn't you say so? Where is she?"

"She left," said Pete. "We didn't know nothing about you two working, so we sent her away."

"Great!" Amber tapped her toe impatiently. "Now I'll have to run her down and tell her the change in plans." She scowled at Pete. "You gonna show me where I'll be working, or not?"

"Come on."

Butterflies fluttered so hard in Amber's stomach that she was sure a few would escape. She walked into the next room with Pete. Two children lay sound asleep or drugged asleep on a wide bed with rumpled covers. Camera equipment and other paraphernalia stood in one corner of the room. The room smelled closed in and dusty. She forced her glance just to pass over the children as she walked around the room. She nodded. "No problem. I've seen all I need to see. I'll be here about noon Thursday."

"Make it three. George is staying here the night, but Keeler and me are leaving and plan to meet back here with Perkins at three Thursday."

Amber nodded. "Three it is. You tell Perkins Weese that I get paid in cash before I start working. He knows what I charge."

"I'll tell him." Pete walked her back to the other room.

Amber turned to Pete and shook her finger at him. "If Betsy comes back, you tell her to meet me here at three Thursday. But don't tell her what the job is. What she don't know ahead of time she can't talk about. Sometimes she talks too much."

"I'll tell her," said Pete.

"I'd sure like to know how the plans got screwed up," said Amber as she walked to the door.

"Too many people in on it," snapped Pete. "I been saying that all along."

"I didn't want in on it," said George gruffly.

"How come?" asked Amber.

Pete glared at George and George only shrugged.

"So don't tell me." Amber waved a hand as if she

couldn't care less. "I didn't let Betsy in on anything for the same reason. And since she doesn't know what I know she doesn't get paid like I do. It all works out." She reached for the doorknob, then turned back. "You guys had better do this job for money up front like me or you might be sorry."

"Why is that?" asked Abe Keeler, rubbing his bald head.

Amber glanced at Pete as if they shared a secret. "Pete knows. So let him explain."

"Hey!" cried Pete. "What do I know?"

"Don't play dumb with me, my man," said Amber with a mischievous chuckle. "I wasn't born yesterday, you know."

"What's she talking about, Pete?" asked Keeler.

"How should I know?" But he looked guilty and George and Abe jumped on that fast, hammering him with questions. Finally Pete stepped away from them and shouted, "Shut up right now! We all get paid Friday just like we agreed. You know we get a bonus for waiting until Friday. And then we're out of here."

"Not me," said Amber with a shrug of her shoulder. "I get paid before the job and then I'm out of here before there's a chance for something to go wrong."

"Go wrong?" cried George. "What could go wrong?"

"Nothing," snapped Pete.

"A lot of things can go wrong with so many people involved," said Amber. "Any time I'm not told who the top dog is in an operation, I get the jitters. It smells like trouble to me."

"Just who *is* the boss?" asked Keeler gruffly.

"None of your business," said Pete, glaring at all of them.

"You told me it was you, Pete," said George. "But it's not, is it?"

"See," said Amber. "Trouble already."

"There'll be more trouble if you don't shut up!" barked Pete.

She flung open the door. "See you Thursday at three. And don't you dare tell Betsy anything!"

"We won't," said Pete impatiently.

Amber walked out the front door, closed it with a firm snap and walked away from the house. She felt as if any minute someone would yell for her to stop. But no one called out and she reached her car safely. She slipped inside and sagged in relief. Perspiration soaked her clothes and made her head itch under the wig. She pulled it off and scratched her damp head.

"So. They get paid Friday. This is Tuesday." She glanced at her watch. "No, Wednesday now." She pulled off the glasses and rubbed her eyes. "Why will Friday be payday for them? What's happening Friday? And since they agreed to wait until Friday they get a bonus. Very interesting."

Finally she stopped shaking enough to pull off her disguise and dress as Amber Ainslie again. She brushed her long red hair until it snapped.

"As soon as George is alone, I'll get the kids," she whispered. She closed her eyes. "Heavenly Father, thank you for helping me find the kids."

Soon she would call Grace and tell her about George. With Sara filing blackmail charges against him, he'd be out of the way. He didn't seem to be as dangerous as Pete Snyder though. Too bad they couldn't force Pete to talk. Finally Amber saw Pete and Keeler drive away. She called Grace, waited several minutes, then ran to the door and knocked. Fear pricked her skin and she forced it away. This was no time to be afraid.

George opened the door and she pushed her way in. "Hello, George."

"Amber Ainslie! What're you doing here?"

"What are *you* doing here? You should be in Ohio, but you're on your way to jail. But first you're going to help me carry those kids to my car."

"What kids?" he asked, nervously looking toward the next room.

"Don't play dumb, George. You're up to your armpits in kiddy porn and you're going to prison for a long time because of it."

George wrung his hands. "Pete stopped me before I could leave. He said I had to stay and help them or he'd kill me. He meant it."

"Too bad you didn't sneak away, George."

He groaned. "I tried to." He held his hand out to Amber, his eyes pleading. "Just let me go now and I promise to head right for Ohio."

"Where's your car?"

He sagged. "Pete took it. He was afraid I'd run."

Before she knew what he was planning, he swung a fist at her. She blocked his blow, caught his arm and flipped him. He landed with a thud flat on his back. She bent down to him, her eyes blazing. "You try anything else and you'll be sorry."

He groaned.

Amber narrowed her eyes. "Tell you what, George. You help me and I'll see that it goes easy on you."

"Help you?" He stood slowly and rubbbed sweat off his face. "How?"

"Help me get the kids to the car."

He shook his head helplessly. "How do you know about the kids?"

"I know a lot of things, George. I even know something big is going down Friday."

"I wish I knew what. All I know is that we get paid that day."

"Why Friday? Why not Thursday after the shoot?"

He shrugged.

She knew he really didn't know. "Let's get the kids."

Defeated, he led the way to the other room and Amber lifted the sleeping girl in her arms while George picked up the boy. They didn't stir and Amber knew they were drugged. They carried them to Amber's car and laid them in the back seat just as Grace Donally stopped her car beside them.

She rolled down her window. "You're under arrest, George Palmer," snapped Grace.

He groaned.

"I tried to help you," said Amber. "You go along with Grace and if you help her she just might get you a lighter sentence."

"Help how?" he asked.

"Tell us who's working the kiddy porn ring."

He named off the men they already knew about.

"Who's the boss?" asked Grace.

"Pete is."

"Give me a break," said Amber. "You know it's not Pete."

"Then who is it?" asked George.

Amber could see he didn't know any more than she did. "Take him in, Grace. I'll get the kids to the hospital."

"You promised they'd go easy with me if I helped you with the kids," George said.

She turned to her car, then turned back. "I did say that, didn't I? Grace, I have a great idea."

"What?" asked Grace.

"What?" asked George in alarm.

"You put George where no one knows about it. Don't tell anyone that isn't absolutely necessary. We'll make it look like he took the kids and left to go into business on his own."

"What?" cried George.

"We'll go back inside and get all the equipment." Amber laughed. "They have a couple of nice video cameras in there. They might even have some tapes that we could take."

"They'll kill me!" cried George.

"And then we'll see what happens," said Amber.

Grace chuckled. "Good idea, Amber. That just might make the big boss get into the action. And we'll be right there to catch him." She called her backup. When the officer drove up she sent him inside to take pictures for later and then move the equipment and any tapes or photos that were there.

Amber turned to George. Suddenly she remembered the Charity Fair Friday. Was there a connection between that and their payday? "Did you hear anyone talk about the Charity Fair Friday?"

George groaned.

"What did you hear, George?" asked Grace sharply.

"I just know that money is involved."

"Were you going to steal the proceeds?" asked Amber.

"No! It's something else. Pete is supposed to turn money over to someone at the Charity Fair so it will look like the Fair took it all in."

"That's strange," said Amber. "Then what?"

"The money is to go to the Burn Center at the hospital." George rubbed his face and the rasp of his whiskers sounded loud in the night air. "That's all I heard about it."

"Porn money was going to build the Burn Center?" asked Amber in shock. "Are you lying, George?"

"It's what I heard," he said in a sharp voice.

"Very strange," said Grace.

Amber opened her car door. "My job is finished now that I've found the kids, but I think I'll stay for the Charity Fair and see what goes on."

A few minutes later she left the children at the hospital and checked on the boy she'd brought Sunday night. He was eating better, the nurse said, but he was still very frightened. Amber stopped in his room and watched him sleep. "Heal his emotional wounds, Jesus," she whispered. "And help him to know that you love him."

Slowly she drove back to her motel room and called Fritz Javor. He sounded half asleep when he answered.

"I knew it was you," he said with a wide yawn. "Can't you call a guy at a decent hour?"

"I tried, but you were *out*."

"I wasn't *out*. I was watching my kid play ball, then I took him home."

"Oh." She sat cross-legged on her bed. "Why is it you always think the worst of me?"

"Is there another side?"

"You hurt me, Red. Hurt me deep."

She laughed. "Sorry, Fritz."

"Were you jealous?"

Suddenly the game was over and she snapped. "What do you have for me?"

"You have nothing to be jealous about, Amber. You're my number one lady."

"Oh, sure." She shook her head and grinned, suddenly feeling better again. "And you're ready to walk down the aisle with me."

"Well, I didn't say that. One time was too much for me. Some people just can't make it in this marriage business."

"Some people need God to help them, Fritz."

"So you keep saying."

"It's true." Amber twisted the phone cord around her finger.

Now it was his turn to get down to business. "I

arrested a distributor of kiddy porn late this afternoon and he wanted to talk real bad, so I let him."

"What did he say?"

"That on Friday he was on his way to some charity fair at Chambers."

"You don't say."

"I thought I just might come on over to the fair and have a look around."

"You have no jurisdiction here."

"I said look around, Red," he said in a hurt voice. "Do I need jurisdiction for that?"

She chuckled. "Than what?"

"I thought I'd meet up with Grace. It's been a while since I saw her. And maybe we'll go to the fair together."

"And what about me?"

"I thought maybe you could be the distributor from here. I kept it quiet about this guy being locked up. I got a man taking care of his business calls." Fritz sat on the edge of his bed with his broad shoulders slumped. He knew he was putting Amber in danger but he knew he could trust her. "Want a new job, Red? It's only for Friday, but the pay is great."

"Fill me in with the details."

Chapter 9

Humming cheerfully, Boyd turned from the stove where he was frying eggs and bacon to see Sara and Carlie walk in. "Good morning," he said. "Ready to eat?"

"I'm hungry," said Carlie as she sat at the table that Boyd had already set. She peeked at Sara. It felt strange to be with her real mom. She was so pretty! Carlie smiled happily.

"Good morning," said Sara. She was surprised at how much at home she felt in Boyd's house.

The toast popped up. Sara buttered it while Boyd put two eggs and two pieces of bacon on each plate. He poured milk for Carlie and tea for himself and Sara.

"Breakfast with my very own daughter," said Sara, kissing the top of Carlie's head. "How I've dreamed of this! It'll be this way from now on."

"Will it really?" asked Carlie with tears glistening in her eyes.

Boyd looked at them with longing. Suddenly he knew the picture wouldn't be complete unless he was in it too. Would Sara feel that way? Or would she insist on marrying Roger Cairns? The thought hurt so much that Boyd had to turn away to keep Sara from seeing his face.

As they finished eating the phone rang. Boyd reached back to the counter behind him and answered it. It was Amber.

"Keep Sara and Carlie at your place today," she said. "Don't let anyone know where they are. Not anyone."

"Sara mentioned that she has to go to work."

"I do," said Sara, nodding.

"She must not!" said Amber. "You tell her. Have her call and tell Rita Hardy that she is away from home. That's the truth. She is away from home. Tell Rita that she'll see her Friday at the Charity Fair."

"I'm helping with that too," said Boyd.

"Oh?"

"Rita asked if I'd take care of the antique auction. I said I would."

Sara looked at him in surprise. She hadn't realized Rita had asked for Boyd's help.

"Tell Sara I'll be over to see her later," said Amber. "You keep them there with you, Boyd. I can't stress enough how important it is."

"I'll do it," he said. He hung up and smiled at Sara and Carlie. "We have the whole day here to ourselves. What shall we do first?"

Sara wanted to ask him what Amber had said, but she didn't want to frighten Carlie. "First, we'll wash the breakfast dishes," Sara said brightly. "And then we could bake cookies."

"Yes!" cried Carlie, laughing. "Just like I saw a

family on TV do!"

"I don't know if I have all the stuff for cookies," said Boyd. But Amber hadn't said he couldn't leave. "We'll make a list and I'll go shopping."

"I'll go with you!" Carlie caught his hand and squeezed it.

"I think you should stay here and talk with your mom," said Boyd. "You have ten years of stories to tell. And your mom can show you her books. They're in my study."

Sara looked at Boyd in surprise. "Do you really have them?"

"Yes. All four. Right on my desk where I can touch them when I want."

His words pleased her more than she cared to admit. She ducked her head and started clearing off the kitchen table.

* * *

Roger paced the kitchen in his small house. Where was Sara? He'd called her until one o'clock this morning, then gave up and went to bed only to toss and turn. He pressed her number again, but she didn't answer. With a groan he called Neddie.

The sound of his voice sent her pulse leaping. "What a pleasant surprise, Roger."

"It's good to hear you too, Neddie. I hope I didn't overstay my welcome last night."

"Not at all. Did you ever reach Sara?"

"No. Have you heard from her?"

"No. But there's nothing strange about that. She has to catch up on her writing since she was gone with Rita Hardy for two weeks."

"You're right. Maybe she turned off her phone and just isn't answering." Roger glanced at his watch. "I'll drive by and see if her car is there. If it is, I'll know that's what she's doing and I'll quit worrying about her."

"Will you call me and let me know?" asked Neddie.

"Yes. Why don't you drop by the store at noon and we'll have lunch together?"

"I'd like that, Roger. See you then."

He didn't want to hang up, but he knew he must. "See you later."

"Later," she whispered.

He hung up and stood with his hand on the receiver. Neddie was going to make some man a good wife. Jealousy ripped through him and he frowned, then rushed to the bedroom to finish dressing.

Later he drove past Sara's small house. Her car was parked in the driveway and he breathed a sigh of relief. After work he would stop by and have a talk with her. He could tell her that he would appreciate knowing when she planned to turn off her phone. Then he wouldn't keep trying to reach her.

At the store he opened the new boxes of books and stocked the shelves. His clerk came in and they talked until the phone rang. Roger answered it.

"Roger, this is Rita Hardy. I've been trying to reach Sara. She's supposed to work today."

He didn't want to let her know Sara had turned off her phone. "She'll probably call you. She's a dependable woman."

"You're right. I guess I was worried for nothing." Rita sighed heavily. "Bob said I should call to make sure she comes to work today."

"I wouldn't worry if I were you."

"I suppose you're right but with the Charity Fair Friday we have a lot to do."

"She'll probably call you."

"Roger, did you notice how tense she was at my party the other night?"

He didn't know how to answer. "I know she was tired."

"Bob thinks that private detective frightened her."

"Sara didn't mention it."

"Then Bob must have been mistaken."

Roger talked a while longer, then Rita rang off. Roger called Neddie and told her about Sara.

"I guess she'll call you later," said Neddie. "Thanks for calling."

"See you at noon."

"Roger, are you sure you want to have lunch with me?"

"Of course!"

"What if Sara calls and wants to see you then?"

"I'll tell her you and I have made plans."

Neddie bit back a moan. She wanted to see Roger but she didn't want to hurt Sara. Was it possible that Boyd was right and Sara didn't love Roger?

"See you at noon, Neddie." He hung up, smiling as he thought about seeing Neddie again soon.

* * *

Amber waited outside the same house as last
night dressed as Tina, the dark-haired photographer
from New York. She drove a small dark blue rented
car that fit into the background. A sparrow hopped
across the yard. A boy on a bicycle rode past. Amber
sighed. She had already been here a couple of hours.
Maybe none of the men would come to check up on
George. She shook her head. Pete would. He
couldn't afford not to since he'd brought George
into it.

About ten Pete pulled into the driveway. To
Amer's relief he was alone. He ran to the door and
knocked, then impatiently pulled out a key and
unlocked it. Amber slipped from her car and silently ran up behind Pete just as he pushed open the
door.

"Pete, I gotta talk to you," she said breathlessly.

He spun around. With a frightened look he pulled
her inside. "What're you doing here today?"

"I had to come." She took a deep breath. "It's
about George."

"George?" Pete frowned as he glanced around.
"George," he called into the silent house.

"He's not here," whispered Amber, shaking her
head. The wind-blown hair slipped like silk across
her slender shoulders. "He left. That's why I'm
here."

Pete ran to the adjoining room and flung wide the
door. He swore, making Amber's ears burn. "He is
gone! The money's gone! The kids are gone. And so is
all the stuff!"

"I know!" Amber plucked at Pete's arm. He wore

the same sweatshirt as last night. "I stopped in again last night to see if Betsy ever came back. George was alone and he was packing stuff like crazy."

Pete slapped his forehead. "That idiot! I tried to call him this morning and, when he didn't answer the phone, I knew I had to get over here."

"He asked if I wanted to go in with him. He took the kids and all the equipment. I begged him not to go, but he said he wanted more than he was getting and the only way to do it was to get out on his own. He said he knew distributors that would take his stuff."

"But how did he leave? I have his car."

Amber shrugged. "He had a light colored Ford, I think. I just figured it was his. When I said I wouldn't go with him he kicked me out." She twisted the rings on her fingers. "I didn't want you thinking I went with him. I don't want it spread around that I don't do my work or I'll never get hired again." She lowered her voice. "I tried to follow him but I lost him over on Pine where it crosses Robins."

"He was leaving town! Heading for the free-way!"

"You tell the boss that it wasn't my fault."

"Man, I don't know what to do." Pete tugged at his straggly hair and dropped to the edge of the couch. "I'll kill that guy when I see him!"

"I don't blame you one bit, Pete."

"I wonder who provided a car for him."

"Could be the fat, bald man that was here last night."

"No. He was with me all night."

"Perkins Weese maybe?"

"I doubt it. But I'll check it out."

"What'll you tell the boss?"

He flopped back in defeat. "I don't know."

Amber walked to the door, then turned. "You could come with me. We could go to Detroit or even on into Canada. Then you wouldn't have to think about what'll happen when the boss hears about George."

Pete jumped up, his eyes wild. "I can't run. There's too much at stake. I'll have to bluff it out."

Amber froze. "Bluff it out?"

"Nobody but you and me knows George took the kids and left. I'll make sure the others don't find out. I'll find a way to get the money. We'll get other kids and we'll get other equipment." Suddenly he laughed. "I still got it!" He gave her a high five and she managed to laugh with him.

"Where will you get kids?"

"I know where some are kept down near the Indiana border. That's where I was headed after Friday."

"Do you think there'd be a job for me?"

"I don't know. We'll talk to Perkins about it."

Amber kept the smile glued in place. She was thankful for the tinted glasses she wore so he couldn't see the sudden fear in her eyes. "Pete, are you driving down to get the kids today?"

"Sure."

"What about the boss? Won't he need to get hold of you?"

Pete rolled his eyes. "You're right."

"I could pick the kids up. You call down, then give me a note to give them so there's no trouble."

"That might work," said Pete thoughtfully. "We might be getting another kid today too. Perkins said he was ready to pick up a girl. I don't know where."

Amber turned away to hide the expression on her face. If it was Carlie Perkins he was talking about, would Pete subject his own daughter to kiddy porn? "Make the call so I can get out of here," she said.

Pete walked to the tiny kitchen where the phone hung on the wall. Amber tried to see what numbers he punched but his arm blocked her view. When he hung up he scribbled a note that nobody could read and she pushed it into her small black purse. He gave her the address and directions. "And you bring them right here. It'll take you about two hours to get there and two back. So I want you here no later than four."

She ran to her car, frantic that the plan with George hadn't worked like she wanted. "But we'll save more kids," she whispered as she drove away.

To make sure she wasn't followed she made several turns that weren't necessary, then pulled quickly into a driveway. She waited but no one drove past so she drove to the nearest pay phone and called Grace. They made arrangements to send a policewoman after the kids. Amber pulled off her disguise, returned the rented car and drove back to her motel. When she didn't show up for the meeting with Pete this afternoon he would be in big trouble. "Serves you right, Pete." she said with a chuckle.

Amber picked up her messages, then stared at one in surprise, her brows raised. "Rita Hardy wants to hire me," Amber said softly. "Now I wonder what this is all about."

Chapter 10

Amber decided to swing past Midge Sawyer's house on the way to see Rita Hardy.

"You said you needed to see me," said Amber as Midge opened the front door. "You look much more rested and relaxed today."

"I am! Come in." Midge led Amber to a small, cozy living room. They sat across from each other in matching loveseats. "I told Ted everything just like you said to do." Midge beamed. "He was very upset at first but then he said he was proud of me for doing something." She squared her shoulders and smiled at Amber. "And he said I should pay you and send you home because the police are taking care of the pornography in this town."

"Oh?" Amber cocked her brow. She hadn't expected that.

"So, here." Midge opened a book on the end table beside her and took out an envelope. "If it's not the right amount, tell me and I'll write another check."

Amber read it in surprise. "It's more than we agreed on."

"I know, but you've been working very hard and I knew you'd be disappointed if you had to leave before the job was finished"

She wanted to tell Midge that the job *was* finished, but she didn't dare let any information leak out before Friday. Amber tucked the check in her purse. "Thank you. I do plan to stay for the Charity Fair Friday."

"That's wonderful!" Suddenly Midge's face fell. "But what if Ted thinks you're still working on the case?"

"We'll just tell him you paid me off."

"Yes. Yes, we'll do that."

"Are you and your husband helping with the fair?"

"Oh, my, yes." Midge smoothed her gray dress slacks over her knees. "I'm helping with the quilt booth. We have some beautiful quilts and so many different designs!"

"And Ted?"

"Ted is selling videos."

Amber sat very still. Was she being overly suspicious? "Videos?"

Midge smiled. "People buy videos and watch them several times, then want to get rid of them. Ted thought of selling them at the fair. People have been donating videos for the last three weeks. We have quite a stack of them. We even put in a few. But I couldn't part with my old movies. I love old movies. Don't you?"

"Yes" Amber crossed her legs and rubbed a hand over her jeans. "Do you suppose I could have a look at the videos?"

Midge frowned slightly. "I'd let you do that,

but Ted said no one is to look at them ahead of time. He said too many people would want ones set aside for them and it would get to be a big hassle."

"But I wouldn't do that. I just want to look at them." Was it possible that kiddy porn videos were hidden among the others?

Midge bit her lower lip and squirmed uncomfortably. "Ted said no one could see them. I'm sure that would include you."

"I could glance over them and Ted would never have to know." Amber could tell that really made Midge nervous.

"I just don't know."

"Where are the videos?"

"Ted has them locked away in a closet in his study. There are thousands of dollars' worth of videos and he got a little nervous having them lay around, he said."

"Have you ever had anyone break into your house?"

"Oh, my, no!" Midge shuddered at the thought.

"But your husband thinks it could happen now?"

Midge picked at her thumbnail, then fingered the beads at her thoat. She looked ready to burst into tears. "I don't believe he thinks that."

"I didn't mean to upset you, Midge. We'll just forget about looking at the videos."

"Oh, that's good!"

Amber jumped up. "I'd better get going, Midge. I'll see you Friday at the fair."

"Are you sure you should stay?"

Amber smiled and patted Midge's shoulder. "It's

a free world, Midge. I can do anything I want."

She sighed in relief. "You're right. Yes, you're right. I'll tell Ted that."

* * *

Several minutes later the maid ushered Amber into Rita Hardy's study. Rita looked up from her phone call. She motioned for Amber to have a seat, then quickly ended her conversation. She walked around to shake hands with Amber. She was almost as tall as Amber. "I'm glad you could come today." Rita was dressed in a dark pink wool suit, a lighter pink silk blouse with a ruffled bow at the neck and black medium-heeled leather shoes. "I was beginning to think you wouldn't make it today, Ms. Ainslie."

"Call me Amber."

"Amber. And I'm Rita." She perched on the arm of the sofa across from Amber.

Amber waited. Some people needed conversation to make them feel at ease. Rita seemed to be one of them. Amber smiled but said nothing.

Sunlight shone through the windows, bathing the room in a gentle warmth. Somewhere outdoors a dog barked.

Rita cleared her throat. "I assume you know why you're here."

"Actually I don't," said Amber.

"Oh, this is very hard." Rita fingered her diamond earring. "You have met Bob, haven't you?"

Amber nodded. "At your party for Sara Palmer."

"Oh, that's right! Sara's a fine person, isn't she?

Did you know her before the party?"

"No." Did Rita want to discuss Sara with her?

"She called this morning to say she was away from home and couldn't come to work."

"Oh?"

"I begged her to come but she said she was sorry. I wonder why she couldn't make it to work. That's not like her at all."

Amber waited. She recognized a fishing expedition when she saw one.

Rita moved restlessly, then sat on the couch and crossed her long legs. "Did you see Sara today?"

"No."

"Yesterday?"

"Could you tell me what this is about?" asked Amber softly.

"Nothing, I guess. It's just that I'm at my wit's end getting ready for the Charity Fair. And to have Sara gone today and tomorrow is too much for me."

"Maybe you could call temporary service for a secretary."

"I might have to." Rita glanced at her desk, her bookcase, then the tall plant rack that held several healthy, green plants.

Amber started to stand. "I really must be going, Rita. I plan to treat myself to a hot fudge sundae."

"Wait! Please don't go."

Amber settled back. She had no intention of leaving before Rita explained why she was here but she didn't want Rita to know that.

"Amber, this is hard for me. I usually don't tell my family secrets to anyone."

Still Amber didn't speak.

Rita jumped up and paced the study. Music from another room drifted in. Suddenly she stopped and leaned back against the desk, her ankles crossed and her hands on the desk on either side of her. "I want you to find out what's bothering my husband. Bob hasn't been himself for almost a month now and the past few days it's been worse. He's quiet and loses his temper easily. And that's not like him at all."

"Maybe he needs to see a doctor. It could be a physical problem."

"It's not. I want you to follow him and see what you can learn."

Amber nodded slightly. Was this really what Rita wanted? Amber felt a little let down.

"You're free to come and go, aren't you?" asked Rita.

"Yes."

"Bob's going out of town tomorrow or Friday and won't be back until Tuesday. Could you find out what he does while he's gone and tell me?"

Amber hid a grin. Was this a real job offer or a way to get her out of town Friday? And if so, why? She knew she would have to play along with Rita. "I'll find out what he does." But she did not need to leave town. She would send Mina on the job. Mina would love it.

"You will be very discreet, won't you Amber?"

"Of course."

"You won't tell Bob?"

"No."

"How do you want to be paid?"

"Half now and half when the job is finished."
Amber named her price and Rita opened her purse and
pulled out cash.

"I don't want Bob to know I hired you, so I must
pay you with cash." .

"That's quite all right." Amber pushed it into
her purse and once again started to stand. She knew
there was more but she wanted to force Rita into
saying it.

Rita held out her hand. "Wait."

Amber settled back.

"Do you think you could take something to Sara
for me?"

"I'm not a messenger service, Mrs. Hardy."

Rita flushed. "I know that. It's just that I have
something urgent to get to Sara. I tried to deliver it
to her. I took it to her home but she wasn't there.
Her car was but she wasn't."

"Then where would I deliver this urgent thing?"

"I thought you might know."

"Me? Her friends might know. I'm only an ac-
quaintance."

"And a detective."

"Oh! You mean you want me to *find* Sara?"

Rita flushed. "It does sound like that, doesn't it?
But I don't mean it to."

"Then I'll be going. I'm sure Friday is soon
enough for you to give her what you have. You did
say she'd be back to work Friday." This time Amber
stood up and took three steps toward the door.

"Please, Amber, don't leave."

Amber turned, her brow cocked. Sunlight turned

her hair to fire.

Rita stood and stepped toward Amber. "I do want you to find Sara. Make sure she's all right. I'm worried about her."

"Is this a job on top of the job of following your husband?"

Rita moistened her lips with the tip of her tongue. "I wouldn't make it that official."

Amber waited, her head tipped slightly, no smile on her face. "Oh."

"Do you think it should be?"

"I'm sure anyone could find Sara. It wouldn't take a detective. Would it?"

"I suppose I could make it official." Rita opened her purse again. "How much do you want?"

"Why don't you pay me after I find her? Did you ever think she might be off with her boyfriend?"

"I called Roger and he doesn't know where she is either."

"What about Neddie?"

"I spoke to her this morning at the bank. She didn't know."

"It sounds like you did a good job of being your own detective." Amber laughed but she saw that made Rita nervous.

"I'd hate to think that Sara is going to work for someone else. She's been a wonderful secretary," Rita said.

"If I can't help you before Friday, then you don't pay me. Does that sound fair?"

Rita frowned. "But I must see her tomorrow! Anyone could find her by Friday. I really want her

today, absolutely no later than noon tomorrow.
I'll double your pay if you can do that."

Amber nodded. "You do want her badly, don't
you?"

"Yes. I suppose I do."

Amber wanted to ask Rita why she couldn't just
say so, but she didn't. "If I don't find her before it's
time to follow your husband, what should I do?"

Rita dropped her purse on the desk and locked her
fingers together. "I hadn't thought of that. I suppose you could follow Bob another time."

So Bob was the ploy and Sara was the real job.
Very interesting. "I'll see what I can do."

"Thank you."

Amber said goodbye and Rita walked her to the
door.

"I would like you to keep this confidential,
Amber. It might be an embarrassment to Sara to
have me send you out scouring the state for her."

"Maybe she went to visit her family." Amber
could hint around for information just as slyly as
Rita had.

"I doubt that."

"What do you know about her past?"

Rita flicked a piece of lint off her sleeve. "She
never talked about her past."

"I could call my office and have my people do a
computer check of her."

"If you think that's necessary."

"I could find out where she went to school, who
her family is, if she has a police record."

Rita nodded. "Yes. Do that. I think I heard her

mention that she has a brother named George."

Amber's heart jerked but she didn't let on, even by the flicker of an eyelash. "Do you want me to check that out too?"

Rita nodded. "You might even find him to see if he knows where Sara is."

Amber could barely stand still. "George." Was Rita trying to see her reaction to George's name? Amber didn't flicker an eyelash.

"Yes. George Palmer." Rita suddenly looked as if she'd just had a very good idea. "In fact, Amber, you find George Palmer as a nice surprise for Sara. I'll pay you a bonus if you find him by tomorrow afternoon."

"You want to surprise Sara. How nice of you." Amber gripped her purse tightly. So, Rita Hardy had hired her to find George! Could it be possible that Rita was involved with Pete and the kiddy porn ring? Or did she, indeed, want to surprise Sara?

Rita patted Amber's arm and whispered, "Now you won't mention it to Sara, will you?"

"Not a word!" Was Rita studying her just a little too intently? Amber managed a conspiratorial smile.

"Good!"

Amber walked to her car and drove away, her head buzzing with wild thoughts.

Chapter 11

Amber leaned back in her motel room chair and propped her feet on the small round table. She heard the sounds of nighttime traffic and a blast of music from someone walking past her door. "Mina, what do you have on Rita and Bob Hardy? And how about Midge and Ted Sawyer?"

"You never told me to check on the Sawyers."

"I know. What'd you find?"

Mina giggled. "Think you're smart, don't you?"

"I know you, Mina."

"Actually, I didn't find anything out of the ordinary on any of them. I really was disappointed."

"Me too. It makes my job harder." Amber had tried to speak to Bob Hardy just after she left Rita, but he wasn't available. His secretary couldn't say when he would be back because he was going out of town on business. "By the way, Mina, I have a job for you that you'll like."

"Oh? I'm all ears!"

"I need you to tail Bob Hardy." Amber told Mina what she knew. Mina said she'd be outside his house early in the morning in her car.

"And don't you worry about him spotting me.

I've even tailed you without your knowing it."

Amber dropped her feet to the floor with a thud. "You what?" she shouted.

"Now, Amber, how am I supposed to learn if I don't practice?"

"I can't believe this!" Amber flipped back her red hair angrily. "Don't you ever follow me again!"

Mina laughed. "Don't worry, Amber. I won't have to. Now that I know how. Anything else?"

"Just keep in touch with me while you're gone. Leave a message here or at the office. If you're really desperate to get me, call Boyd Collier. You already have his number. I'll check in with him regularly." Amber started to sign off, then said, "Did you look at the house?"

"Yes. It's not what we want. It needed too many repairs and it was much too large."

"After I get home I'll look around for myself."

"Fine. If that's the way you want to be. But I thought that was my job." Mina sounded as if her feelings were hurt. "I thought you wanted me to take that load off your shoulders."

Amber smiled and shook her head. "Drop the act, Mina. Pretending you have hurt feelings won't keep me from checking around for a place."

"Just so you find one big enough for both of us," said Mina sharply.

"Talk to you soon, Mina." With a laugh Amber hung up. She glanced at her watch. Was it too late to talk to Ted Sawyer? She'd tried meeting with him earlier but he said Wednesdays were too busy for him because of Wednesday night church. Was he trying to avoid her? "Maybe I'm just overly suspicious," she muttered as she dialed Sawyer's home number. Midge answered.

"It's Amber Ainslie, Midge. May I speak to your husband?"

"Ted?"

"Yes." Did she have more than one husband?

"He...he is going to bed and doesn't want to talk...to...anyone."

Amber frowned. "Midge, is he upset that I want to speak to him?"

"Yes," she said just above a whisper.

"Why?"

"I don't know."

"Or you can't say. Is that it?"

"My husband says it's time for me to go to bed, too. Good night, Amber."

Amber slowly hung up then paced the room, her hands locked behind her back. Suddenly she stopped. "Grace Donally! I'll see what she thinks about this. She said Pastor Sawyer offered help and information to her."

Amber called Grace at home and they talked several minutes. Finally Grace said, "I suppose Ted Sawyer feels that the police should handle this. Maybe he doesn't care for private detectives."

"Maybe."

"He has cooperated with me, Amber."

"Did you know he was in charge of selling used videos at the Charity Fair?"

"No. Is that supposed to mean something?"

"Do you realize how easy it would be to slip in

kiddy porn? It could be disguised as a regular movie."

"You're right. I'll check into it."

Amber twisted a long lock of hair around her finger. "Grace, why don't you take a few videos to Ted as donations and, while you're there, see if he will show you the ones he's collected. If he won't, then tell him it's police business and you must see them. That should answer some questions."

"He's a nice man, Amber."

"I know. Do it anyway."

"You're right, of course. Don't you feel like you have a heart of stone at times?"

"Yes. Yes, I do. But that comes with the territory."

"You're so right."

"What's the word on the kids down by the Indiana border that you sent your officer to pick up?"

"Safe. They're in a hospital in Niles." Grace sighed tiredly. "Their bodies are free but not their minds. Who can erase from their memories all they've been through?"

"Only a miracle from God," said Amber softly.

"I pray someone who knows that will be there for them," said Grace. She was quiet a long time, then said, "Hey, by the way, Fritz Javor called a while ago. He's coming Friday morning and will meet me at the fair about nine. He said it's to look like a date so nobody gets suspicious. But he also said it wasn't a real date. He wanted you to know."

Amber rolled her eyes. Trust Fritz to know when to say the wrong thing. "Thanks, Grace."

"Is there something going with you two?"

"No. We're just friends."

"Oh. I guess maybe Fritz doesn't know that."

Amber said something to make Grace laugh and quickly hung up. Sometimes she wished there was something between her and Fritz, but she knew there never could be as long as he wasn't a born-again Christian. "Father, in Jesus' Name, show Fritz that you love him. Send believers across his path to tell him about you. And, Father, I'm open to be used. I will never be ashamed to talk to him about you." Tears slipped down her cheeks as she continued to intercede for Fritz.

* * *

Her icy hands locked behind her back, Sara paced Boyd's living room. He had gone out for milk and Carlie was fast asleep in her room. Sara stopped abruptly. *"Her room?* I can't start thinking like that!" Oh, but it was so easy to do.

Being with Boyd last night and all day today had brought back emotions that she thought were dead. It was so easy to feel like a complete family—Carlie, Boyd and her.

Just where did Roger fit into her life?

"Roger!" How could she forget about him?

She ran to the phone and called his number. Why hadn't she let him know that she was safe? She knew he would be worried about her. She always let him know when she would be away and how long she planned to be gone.

He answered immediately and she sighed in relief. He sounded so...so like Roger.

"Hi, Roger."

"Sara! I've been frantic!" He sank to the chair beside the phone. He had just hung up after talking with Neddie. "Frantic! So has Neddie."

"I'm sorry, Roger. My life is sort of upside-down right now."

"Why?"

"It's a long story."

"I'll come right over and we can talk."

"Roger, I'm...not...at...home."

He frowned. "Where are you?"

She closed her eyes and leaned against Boyd's desk. Roger would never understand, would he? "With a friend."

"Let's meet somewhere."

"I really can't." She opened her eyes and saw her books on Boyd's desk. They sat in a place of honor as if they were important to him. Roger hadn't read anything she'd written. He said if he read the back covers, that was enough to help him sell the books.

"I must see you *now*, Sara. Now, tonight!"

She sighed raggedly. "I am staying at Boyd Collier's house."

"Boyd Collier's?" cried Roger, suddenly so angry his face turned brick red. "Why?"

"I can't explain."

"I'll be right over."

"No!"

"I'm coming right over, Sara."

"All right." With a moan she hung up the phone and paced the room again. She jumped when Boyd walked in.

"What's wrong?" he asked. "You're pale and you look ready to cry."

"I just called Roger." She crossed her arms and rubbed the sleeves of her raspberry red sweater. "He is very upset."

"And?"

"He's coming over."

Jealousy ripped through Boyd. "Just call him right back and tell him to stay away!"

"I can't. He's been worried about me."

Boyd gripped her arms. "Sara, I don't want that man in this house! I mean it!"

"Why? I thought you liked Roger."

He dropped his arms and spun away from her to look out into the darkness of the backyard. How could he explain it to her?

With trembling hands Sara hooked her hair behind her ears. "I know this is your home, Boyd. I had no right to have Roger come, but he insisted. I do owe him an explanation of my silence." She cleared her throat. "And I must tell him about Carlie."

"That should be interesting," Boyd said drily as he turned to face Sara. "Just what do you think straight-laced Roger will do about Carlie?"

Sara lifted her chin. "Probably just what you did eight years ago. Get angry and walk away."

Boyd jammed his hands into his jeans pockets and hunched his broad shoulders. "Will you ever forgive me for that?"

"Yes. Yes, I did forgive you, Boyd."

"I was *so* wrong!"

"Yes, you were," said Sara just above a whisper. "Are you prepared if Roger walks out on you?"

"Yes. I have my daughter. I can be happy with just the two of us if I must."

With the grace of a panther, Boyd sprang forward and caught her close to his heart. "You don't have to be alone, Sara. You and Carlie will always have me."

His touch melted her very bones. The yearning on his face sent her senses reeling. She pushed against his chest. "Don't! Let me go, Boyd."

"I can't!"

"You must!"

"I let you go eight years ago. I can't do it again."

She moaned and weakened, swaying against him.

The doorbell chimed and she broke Boyd's hold. "That's Roger."

Boyd stabbed his fingers through his hair. "Send him away."

"I must talk to him, Boyd."

Struggling with his feelings, he finally said, "I'll go to my room." He ran a finger down her cheek. "But we'll finish our talk after he leaves."

She trembled and went to answer the door.

Roger stepped inside and stared at her intently. "You look very different," he said hoarsely. "What has happened?"

She pushed back her chestnut-brown hair and fingered the gold chain around her neck. "Let's have a cup of coffee and talk."

"I didn't come for coffee." He was usually a very

patient man but he had lost all patience where Sara was concerned. "Tell me why you're here."

"I needed a safe place to stay," she said hesitantly.

"Then why didn't you come to me?"

"I...I never thought of it."

"But you thought of Boyd Collier, your old friend." A muscle jumped in Roger's jaw.

"He was there, Roger."

"There?"

"I...I can't really explain that easily. Please, let's sit down and talk. You're making me very nervous."

He tipped his head in agreement.

She led him to Boyd's music room. She dare not take him to Boyd's study or the room she'd pictured as her study.

The music room held a baby grand piano, a sound system, comfortable chairs and a sofa. Sara clicked on the lamp. It cast a soft glow over the piano and around the room. Earlier Carlie had fun trying to play the piano. Nervously Sara thought about her dream of Carlie taking lessons and really learning to play.

Roger walked around like a caged tiger. He wasn't used to feeling so frustrated and angry. What had happened to his ordinary life? His plan was to marry Sara and live a quiet, happy life. The greatest anguish he'd ever had was when he was late with a bank payment a couple of years ago.

"Please sit down, Roger," said Sara as she sat on a soft chair that seemed to hold her protectively close. Searching for a way to tell him her news, she wanted to reach out and comfort him. Instead she folded her hands over her crossed knees and waited for him to sit.

"Where is Boyd Collier?"

"In his room. He knew we needed privacy."

Finally Roger unbuttoned his suit coat and leaned back as he looked at Sara. "Well?"

"Roger, it's a long story and I know you must be tired. It is late."

"I am tired. But I want to hear what you have to say."

"You already know that Boyd and I knew each other before he came here."

Roger nodded.

"I was a foster child and Boyd's parents took me in and loved me as their own." Oh, how could she tell him what her life had been like before that point? She searched for words. "My real family had a lot of problems. My mother kicked me out. My brothers have been in and out of jail."

Roger tugged at the knot of his tie. "What does your past have to do with your staying here?"

"My brother...my brother, George, was trying to blackmail me because of my past. It was safe to come here away from...from George."

Just then Carlie ran into the music room, her feet bare and her cotton nightgown flapping around her thin legs. "Mom, where were you? I looked all over." She ran to Sara and jumped into her lap.

"I wouldn't leave you, Carlie." Sara held Carlie close and kissed the top of her head.

Roger's mouth dropped open as he watched Sara reassure Carlie. He listened in shock as they talked. Finally Carlie snuggled against Sara and dropped off to sleep again.

"Sara?" Roger whispered hoarsely.

In a low voice that often broke Sara told Roger about Carlie and Pete, the agony of losing Carlie, and what led up to staying with Boyd. She did not tell him that she had been desperately in love with Boyd or that he forced her to leave his parents' home after high school. "Well, Roger? Are you going to walk out and never speak to me again?"

"Of course not! I'm just surprised. Shocked is probably a better word." Roger grinned weakly. "It's quite a story. I suppose I can understand why you're here and why you didn't think to call me."

"Good." Sara smiled in relief. "I was petrified when George first called me. I thought he would tell you everything and you'd hate me forever."

"Does Neddie know any of this?"

"No."

"She'll still love you, Sara. None of this will make her stop caring."

Tears sparkled in Sara's eyes. "I guess I really needed to trust you both, didn't I?"

"Yes." Roger walked over to Sara and knelt beside her chair. "You have a beautiful little girl. I am glad for you that you finally have her back."

"Me too."

Roger kissed Sara gently. "I'll see you again tomorrow."

"Remember, you can't tell anyone about my being

here. And don't tell anyone about Carlie. I'll tell people in my own way and my own time."

Sara carefully laid Carlie on the sofa and covered her with an afghan, then slipped her arms around Roger. "Thank you."

"For what?"

"For being understanding."

"No problem." He kissed her cheek. "I must be going. I guess it was a good thing you didn't come to my place. It's too small for three of us."

Sara chuckled. "I guess it is." She hugged him tightly. "You're a nice man, Roger."

"Thanks. I wondered about myself. I thought maybe you didn't care about me any longer."

"I care!"

He held her close and said against her hair, "Neddie will be so glad that you're all right."

Just then Sara glanced up. Boyd stood in the doorway, his face pale and his eyes filled with pain. She jumped away from Roger. "Boyd, we didn't hear you."

"So it seems." He glanced at the sofa. "I went to check on Carlie and, when she wasn't there, I got a little concerned. But I see she's just fine."

Roger stepped forward, his hand out. "Boyd, thanks for being such a good friend to Sara and her daughter."

Boyd shot a look at Sara, then shook Roger's hand. Boyd really wanted to toss Roger out on his ear. He pushed back the terrible thought and managed to answer Roger in a civilized manner. "I'm glad I was here to help." He walked to the sofa and gently lifted Carlie in his arms. "I'll tuck her back in bed."

"Thank you," said Sara as she locked her trembling hands behind her back and turned her flushed face away. She didn't want Boyd to notice how guilty she felt for being in Roger's arms. And why should she feel guilty? She and Roger were going to talk about marriage—and would have if her life hadn't suddenly turned upside-down.

Sara watched Boyd walk away with Carlie, then she turned to Roger. "I must stay here at Boyd's for a while longer, but we'll talk again when I get home."

Roger nodded. "I'll probably see you Friday at the Charity Fair."

"Yes."

"Neddie and I are going together. I know you'll be busy."

Sara nodded. "Neddie will be very surprised about Carlie."

"She will. But she loves you and won't judge you. After all, that all happened before you were born again. You were made a new creature in Christ when you accepted Jesus as your Savior. So you are the Sara we know and love."

Sara blinked back tears. "Thank you. I guess I never thought it through, but I do know that I am a new person. It's hard to realize that *I* was Sara Noreen Palmer, the girl who grew up in a terrible family, the teen who had a baby and was tossed out of her home." She laughed softly. "Now I'm a successful writer, a Christian and I have my baby back!" She clasped her hands under her chin and her eyes sparkled happily. "Not even being frightened or having to hide out can steal my happiness."

"I'm glad." Roger took her hand. "Walk me to the door. I must get home and let you go to bed."

"I am tired."

At the door he hugged her, then walked out. She stood in the doorway until his taillights disappeared down the street. The cool breeze felt good against her warm skin. She smelled exhaust fumes in the air as well as a hint of after-shave. She turned and bumped into Boyd. It was his after-shave.

He closed and locked the door and stood against it, his arms crossed. The light from the wall sconce cast a warm glow over the entry hall. "So I see he didn't rant and rave and walk out on you."

"No. He didn't." She looped her fingers in her jeans pockets. "And I'm glad, too."

Boyd sighed heavily. "Yes, me too. I didn't want you hurt more."

"Thank you."

"Would you like milk and cookies before we go to bed?"

She grinned and tossed her head. She didn't want to leave him until she knew the agony she'd seen on his face earlier was gone. "Sounds great. Let's go."

Chapter 12

Amber glanced at Grace Donally who sat behind the desk in her office, then handed the phone to George. Grace held another phone to her ear so she could hear the conversation. "You say exactly what I told you to say to her, George."

"I said I would, didn't I?" George hated being locked up again. Right now he would do anything to get out and go straight. He should have grabbed the chance Amber gave him to leave instead of letting Pete talk him into staying.

"Didn't she answer yet?" asked Amber, tapping her toe impatiently. She gripped the back of George's chair as she looked at her watch. Thursday noon.

George leaned forward at the sound of the voice. "Mrs. Hardy, George Palmer here. I understand you're looking for me."

Rita bit back a gasp and sank to her office chair. "Yes, George. Where are you?"

"Does it matter?"

"No. I just need to meet with you."

"It's not safe for me to be in Chambers."

"Why is that, George?"

"You don't want to know." His palms were so sweaty the phone slipped in his hand. "I heard that that private detective, Amber Ainslie, was looking for me."

Rita pressed her hand to her stomach. "Did you hear why?"

"No." What if she asked him something that Amber hadn't given him the answer to?

"I believe you have something of mine."

"Not that I know of. You tell me what you want or I'm hanging up right now. I got things to do."

"Wait! Listen, George, you took the equipment and the...the..."

"Wait a minute!"

"Don't deny it, George. Pete Snyder told me. You took everything." Rita trembled and glanced at her closed office door. It would be terrible if Bob walked in now. He knew nothing about her unusual way of making money. And he wouldn't approve, no matter what she said. "George, I'm ready to make a deal."

"What kind of deal?"

Amber raised her hands in victory.

Rita swallowed hard. "You may keep the...subjects and the equipment, but I need the cardboard box marked 'tapes.' It's about the size of a boot box. And I need it back today."

"I didn't notice no box marked tapes." He looked helplessly at Amber.

She turned to Grace, her brow raised questioningly.

Grace ran a finger down the list of things taken from the house. She found it listed and nodded. She handed Amber the phone and slipped out to get it.

"But it's gone from the house, George. Who else would have taken it?"

"Pete maybe?"

"He didn't. Now, George, you check over the things again and see if you have it."

"You want me to call you back or what?"

"No. I'll wait. But please hurry!"

George covered the mouthpiece and turned to Amber. "She's scared," he whispered. "She says she has to have that box today."

She covered her mouthpiece. "I heard. Maybe the box contains the masters."

George shrugged. "I doubt it."

Grace slipped back into the room and opened the box. "Tapes," she whispered in disappointment.

Amber looked closely at the box, pulled the tapes out and lifted a false bottom. She bit back a gasp. It was full of fives, tens, twenties and a tidy stack of fifties. She had never expected money—masters, yes, to be turned into money as they were duplicated and sold, but never cash. Pete had mentioned that George had taken the money. But she didn't dream it was this kind of money.

George stared at the money. If he could grab it and run, he would.

"My, my," said Grace, still inspecting the money.

"Tell her you found the box but didn't open it," whispered Amber.

"I got the box," he said into the phone.

"Good. Did you open it?"

"No."

"Please don't. Bring the box to me."

"Now? I can't do that."

"Send it special messenger, then."

"Why should I? You don't have no way to make me, so I'll just keep it with the other stuff."

"I worked too hard to get it!" snapped Rita, dabbing perspiration off her face with a tissue. She and Pete were the only ones who had known about the box of money. She needed it tomorrow at the Charity Fair. "If you don't get that box to me, George, I will have you killed. Do you understand me? I can find you easily, George, and you will be dead. Just like Olga Swensen. Did you read about her accident in the paper, George? It can happen to you too, no matter how far you run or how much you try to hide."

Grace heard and her eyes flashed with anger.

George rubbed his jaw. Even though he knew he was safe, she still scared him out of his wits. "I'll get it to you."

"See that you do, George. If it's not here before three o'clock this afternoon, you're a dead man."

Grace scribbled a quick note and passed it to George. He read it and said to Rita, "I can't get it there today. Would tomorrow be all right?"

"Oh, all right! But you make sure it's here. Eight o'clock in the morning. Leave it at the video booth with Ted Sawyer." Rita slammed down the receiver and leaned back, totally exhausted. She really should not have said all of that to George over the phone, but he had frightened her so badly that she'd lost it for a while.

Grace told Amber what Rita had said. "I never would have suspected that lady of any of this. She's so nice and she does so many wonderful things."

"Like raising money for the Burn Center," said Amber drily. "Fritz said the distributor was to be at the Fair to bid on antiques with money that someone was going to give him there. We couldn't understand what was going on."

"We do need that Burn Center." Grace jumped up and paced her office. "But we do *not* want kiddy porn money in it. Just what is going on here? I've never heard of such a thing! And just what does Ted Sawyer have to do with all of this?"

George eyed the money and almost drooled.

Amber thoughtfully tapped her chin with her finger. In her judgment, Ted Sawyer had acted very suspicious. Even if Grace didn't want to admit it, maybe he was involved.

Grace dropped to her chair. "Now we can arrest Pete and the others. We have you, Amber, and George here to testify against them and we have the proof of what they were doing."

"And the kids are safe," said Amber.

"I'm thankful for that!" Grace pushed up her jacket sleeves. "Rita Hardy sounds like the top guy we've been looking for."

"Yes," said Amber grimly. "But there are others working with her. If that one distributor will be there, others will too. We'll have to be at the

Charity Fair."

"We'll take the money to the fair and see what happens," said Grace. She laughed. "Of course, it will be marked so we'll know where it goes if some of it accidently slips through our fingers."

"I've noticed you didn't say a word about Ted Sawyer."

Grace tapped the tips of her fingers together. "I have faith in that man, Amber. But I will keep an eye on him."

"And so will I," Amber added silently.

* * *

Friday morning Sara Palmer stood at Boyd's kitchen window. After today she and Carlie would go back to her place to live. A strange loneliness rose up inside her. She bit the inside of her lower lip to keep from crying.

What was wrong with her? She should be happy. She and Roger were as close as ever even though he knew about her past and about Carlie.

Sara watched a robin hop across the grass. She and Boyd had resolved the pain of eight years ago and were friends.

"Friends?" she whispered huskily. After spending the past four days with him, it would be hard to release that part of her life.

She heard him call to Carlie, then Carlie giggled as they played together. "She loves him too," said Sara.

Her eyes widened and she clamped her hand over her mouth as she realized what she had said.

Did she love Boyd?
She did!

Tears filled her eyes as she whimpered. How could that happen? For eight years she'd hated him.

But had she really? Had the hatred been only a false covering to hide her hurt? Had her love been there all the time, tucked away in a hidden place in her heart where nothing could destroy it?

With a moan she sank to the edge of a kitchen chair.

Just then a squealing Carlie ran into the room. Boyd was close behind her calling,"I'll catch you yet Carlie!"

"Save me, Mom! Save me!" cried Carlie, laughing as she ducked behind Sara's chair.

"She can't save you," said Boyd, laughing as he swooped down on both of them. He encircled them with his arms and pushed his face into Carlie's neck. She giggled and squirmed and almost tipped the chair over.

Sara burst out laughing and pushed against Boyd. Love for him seemed to spring from every pore in her body. She and Boyd and Carlie were so right. They belonged together. Roger had no place in her life—no place at all. Suddenly she understood that as if she'd received the message written in the sky.

Boyd lifted his face and saw the look in her eyes. His heart leaped. "I love you," he mouthed.

Carlie wriggled away and pushed Boyd back. He was off balance enough that it sent him in a heap on the floor. Carlie jumped on him and they laughed together.

Sara sat very still and watched them. Had she read his lips correctly? Or had he mouthed something else and she only imagined it to be that he loved her?

Boyd jumped up with Carlie high in his arms. "Carlie, I want to talk to your mom in private. Could you go read a book or watch TV or something?"

"Sure." Carlie looked at them nervously. "You gonna fight?"

"No," said Boyd. "Don't you worry about that. I'll shout when we're finished."

"It's almost time to go to the Charity Fair," said Sara, her nerves tingling as she wondered what Boyd wanted to talk about.

"There's plenty of time," said Boyd. "Run along, Carlie." He kissed her cheek and stood her up.

She looked helplessly at Sara. Sometimes she thought she had fallen asleep and dreamed the past few days. It seemed too good to be true that she was with her real mom.

Sara pulled her close and kissed her. "Go on. It's all right."

"You don't want to give me away again, do you?"

"No!" cried Sara holding Carlie even tighter.

"She never wanted to, Carlie," said Boyd softly. "She was forced to. And nobody can force her to do that again."

"Never," said Sara against Carlie's soft hair so much like her own. "You will live with me until you're old enough to have a home of your own."

"I'll never move away from you!" said Carlie.

Sara smiled as she held Carlie's face between her hands. "Some day you will want to have a husband and a family. But I'll still be a part of your life. I always, always will be."

A few minutes later Boyd and Sara stood alone in the kitchen. The hum of the refrigerator seemed loud in the sudden silence. The smell of toast hung in the air. She turned to look out of the window. She couldn't look at his face in case she had read the message wrong.

Gently he turned her toward him. His touch burned into her skin. "Sara, I love you," he said softly.

"You can't." she whispered.

"I do."

"Is it possible?" she said around a lump in her throat.

"I love you and I want to spend the rest of my life with you and with Carlie."

"Oh, Boyd!"

He pulled her close and kissed her gently, then hungrily. She clung to him returning his kisses with a passion she thought was dead.

Finally he lifted his head and looked deep into her eyes. She felt as if she was drowning. "I love you, Sara Noreen Palmer."

"I love you," she whispered brokenly. Dare she trust him? Would he suddenly remember who she was and push her away with words of anger?

He saw the sudden pain in her eyes and it made him uneasy. "Sara, will you marry me?" he asked hesitantly.

"Do you mean it, Boyd?" she questioned in a tiny voice.

He nodded. "I will always love you. I promise." He gently kissed her. "Will you marry me?" he asked against her mouth.

"Yes," she answered back. "Yes!"

* * *

Rita Hardy stopped inside the tent that was set aside for the Charity Fair office. People were already swarming the huge fairgrounds. Rita smiled. It was going to be a great success. For a short time she had been afraid things wouldn't work out. But when she picked up the box from Ted Sawyer, she was confident that he didn't know what was inside. She didn't see George Palmer deliver it but that was to her advantage. She didn't want anyone connecting her with George, especially now that Pete and the others had been arrested. She knew Pete would keep her identity a secret just as he had the last time he was arrested. She had provided a good lawyer for him and promised him a job when he was out again. She breathed a sigh of relief. Things always went her way because she wasn't greedy and she was patient.

Opening her briefcase, Rita dropped part of the money inside, locked it and set it under the counter. That was her pay. She stuffed the rest of the money into envelopes that she had brought. That money would go toward building the Burn Center. As long as she continued to do good with part of her money, she knew she was safe. This money would assure that the Burn Center would be built this year. Why, she could look around town as well as neighboring towns and see all the good that she'd done. Sharing her profits was fun and left her with a good feeling. If the others had shared their earnings they would be as free and happy as she was.

Amber walked in disguised as Tina. With Pete and the others locked away, she knew no one would know her. "I know I'm early but I saw a quilt I wanted. I'd hate to see someone else get it."

Rita Hardy looked up with a smile. "Good morning."

"It's a fine day for a fair." What stupid pass words! Amber held out the card that Fritz had given her from the distributor he'd arrested. Rita looked at it and handed Amber an envelope of money.

"Bid up the items at the auction," said Rita. "I want this money used by the end of the day."

"I can handle that. I saw a couple of quilts I'd like to buy."

"There are some beautiful quilts, aren't there?"

Amber wanted to wring Rita's neck but she kept a smile on her face. "There certainly are."

Grace Donally and Fritz Javor walked in. He was tall and broad with thinning brown hair and keen blue eyes. He wore jeans with a matching jacket and a red plaid shirt.

Amber bit back a smile. Would Fritz recognize her?

Rita whispered, "Police. Don't talk to them."

Amber stood to one side as Grace walked right up to Rita. Fritz stopped at Amber's side. He lifted a brow but she looked away.

"Good morning, Rita," said Grace. "It's a fine day for a fair."

Rita's eyes widened.

Grace held out the same kind of card that Amber had.

"What is this all about?" asked Rita, her mouth dry.

Bob Hardy walked into the tent with Mina on his heels. "Don't you recognize the card, Rita?" he asked coldly.

Her face turned ashen. "I don't know what you mean, Bob."

Mina glanced at Amber then looked again. Mina knew it was Amber but she didn't say a word and Amber was thankful.

Bob sank heavily to a folding chair. "I began to suspect you were doing something illegal a couple of months ago, but I never dreamed it was...was kiddy porn. Rita, how could you? You love kids!"

"Please, don't do this," said Rita, tears filling her eyes. "It'll ruin the Charity Fair."

"Too bad you didn't think of that sooner," said Grace.

"I'm sure the fair will go on without your help," said Bob. "Sara can easily handle your job here at the fair. In fact, she already knows she'll be doing it. I told her."

Rita hung her head.

Grace touched her hand. "Rita, why? I can't understand why you became involved in pornography. You don't need the money and you seem to have a wonderful life."

"Didn't I give you enough?" asked Bob brokenly.

"Never a child!" cried Rita. "And it wasn't fair!"

"You're under arrest, Rita," said Grace raggedly. "Mason will take your place in here and will arrest each person who comes in for a packet of money."

As four plainclothes officers walked into the tent, Amber dropped the packet of money on the counter and walked away.

Fritz caught her arm. "Just where do you think you're going?" he asked.

She lowered her glasses and said, "Home probably."

He chuckled. "Come on. I'll ride with you." He turned to call to Grace. "Talk to you later."

"I'll come too," said Mina.

"Not on your life," said Fritz with a look that stopped Mina in her tracks.

* * *

Sara stood to the side of the ticket booth, still unwilling to believe what Amber had told her about Rita Hardy. Sara shuddered as she realized how many times she had helped Rita filter money from pornography into her good works.

"But you had no way of knowing," Boyd had said with his arm protectively around her.

She glanced around to see where he took Carlie. Instead of Boyd and Carlie she saw Roger and Neddie walking arm in arm, deep in conversation. "They *do* love each other," Sara whispered in surprise. Trust Boyd to be right.

Sara stepped forward and called, "Roger. Neddie. Hi."

Blushing, Neddie stepped away from Roger but he caught her hand and led her to Sara.

Sara hugged them both. "Roger, you may tell Neddie my deep, dark secret now. And introduce her to Carlie when you run across her and Boyd."

"Carlie?" asked Neddie with a slight frown.

"I'll explain," said Roger.

Sara took a deep breath. "Now I have to tell you both something that might surprise you. Please don't be angry with me. Especially you, Roger."

"What is it?" he asked.

"Hold his hand, Neddie," said Sara softly.

Neddie did.

Sara squared her shoulders and wiped her hands down her jacket. "I am going to marry Boyd Collier."

"What?" Neddie and Roger both cried at once.

"I am. And I want you both to be happy for me because I am happier than I've ever been." Sara touched Roger's hand. "You and I love each other, Roger, but it's a friendship love, not a love for marriage. Look in your heart. You'll know it is true."

"She's right, Roger," said Neddie, looking into his eyes with her love for him shining through. She turned to Sara. "Thank you!"

Finally understanding, Roger slipped his arm around Neddie where he knew it belonged.

* * *

Boyd watched Carlie ride one more time on her favorite ride. He pulled Sara close to his side. "It seems like she's always been with us, doesn't it?"

Sara nodded. "I've missed the first ten years of Carlie's life, but it will be full of love from now on." Sara looked up at Boyd. "I'm glad you found me."

"Me too. I almost gave up looking but God was there nudging me on to find you."

Tears sparkled in Sara's eyes. "He is truly a miracle worker."

* * *

Amber leaned back against the booth and smiled at Fritz. "Thanks for the hot fudge sundae."

"You are very welcome. I have another gift for you too."

"You do? What?"

He handed her a brown paper bag. "Excuse the beautiful wrapping paper."

She peeked inside. "A video?"

He chuckled. "And it's legitimate."

"I know it would be," she said soberly.

"I'm aware that you thought maybe Ted Sawyer was involved but he wasn't. He just doesn't like private investigators and he took his job with the video sales very seriously."

Amber slowly pulled the video out and looked at the cover. "Fritz! Thank you! It's Charlie Chaplin."

"I know. Your favorite."

Amber chuckled and shook her head. "No. He's

your favorite. I like Fred Astair and Ginger Rogers."

Fritz slapped his forehead. "That's right! How could I forget?" He pulled another video from a bag on the seat beside him and held it out to her. "Here you go. Fred Astair and Ginger Rogers at their best."

She laughed and took it.